'Don't make ███
Erin.

'Because, damn it ███ to play this as straight and fair as I can. I've come out here with my son. I'm offering you my life, and I've burned my bridges. Meet me halfway.'

She stiffened, pushing her palms hard against his chest.

He let her go, and she stepped back.

He said, suddenly bleak, 'So this is all a mistake, then? You don't love me. I've come all this way. I want you and need you so much. Have done for two years and more. And you're turning me away.'

'No, of course I love you! But does that make you happy? I loved you, still, when I hadn't seen you in more than two years, when I saw you at your own wedding, when I hadn't even met your child. But if you think that solves everything then you're so wrong.'

Lilian Darcy is back in her native Australia with her American historian husband and their four young children. More than ever, writing is a treat for her now, looked forward to and luxuriated in like a hot bath after a hard day. She likes to create modern heroes and heroines with good doses of zest and humour in their make-up, and relishes the opportunity that the medical series gives her for dealing with genuine, gripping drama in romance and in daily life. She finds research fascinating too—everything from attacking learned medical tomes to spending a day in a maternity ward.

Recent titles by the same author:

THE PARAMEDIC'S SECRET
A NURSE IN CRISIS
THE TRUTH ABOUT CHARLOTTE

MIDWIFE
AND MOTHER

BY
LILIAN DARCY

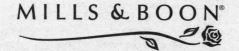

MILLS & BOON®

All the characters in this book have no existence outside the imagination of the author, and have no relation whatsoever to anyone bearing the same name or names. They are not even distantly inspired by any individual known or unknown to the author, and all the incidents are pure invention.

First published in Great Britain 2001
Harlequin Mills & Boon Limited,
Eton House, 18-24 Paradise Road, Richmond, Surrey TW9 1SR

© Lilian Darcy 2001

ISBN 0 263 82699 6

Set in Times Roman 10¼ on 11½ pt.
03-1101-52827

Printed and bound in Spain
by Litografia Rosés, S.A., Barcelona

CHAPTER ONE

'THIS can't be a coincidence!' Erin Gray muttered, half under her breath and half to the third-year resident who had just entered Room Two of the birth suite at Black Mountain Hospital.

'No, of course it isn't, but we can't talk about it now,' came the resident's strained response.

'No, obviously not,' she replied, then fled the delivery room. The Perspex infant cot rattled on its rubber wheels in front of her.

Thank goodness for this errand! She was weak and shaky all over, her heart was pounding, there was a ringing in her ears, she felt a lot older than her twenty-eight years and she was hot, *hot* from head to toe, as if someone had suddenly plunged her under a high-voltage heat lamp.

She parked the cot in the corridor and took a second, more sophisticated neonatal resuscitation trolley to wheel into the delivery room, fighting to keep the flood of churning emotion at bay.

Can I take a moment? Just thirty seconds or so, before I go back in? she wondered, hanging onto the resus. trolley as if it was her own life support, not the imminent baby's. Oh, Lord, I *have* to! That's Alec in there. *Here!* Alec Rostrevor. Resident on call in my hospital, at eleven forty-five on a Monday night, when he's supposed to be halfway around the world in London, married to beautiful Kate. What happened?

Through the open doorway of Delivery Room Two, she heard the labouring woman moan again. 'I don't see the point of this! It's awful. I hate that nurse!'

She didn't mean Erin, but no-nonsense Tricia Gallant.

5

Tricia had ended her shift forty-five minutes ago, just after assuring her patient that there was no time to summon the anaesthetist to administer an epidural.

'I hate her! I wanted that epidural!'

By now, however, it really was too late. Sandra Taylor was fully dilated and ready to push. Her dark hair was a messy bush framing her face and the skin around her eyes and mouth were stretched tight with pain. But there were potential problems developing. Erin had broken her patient's waters several minutes ago, and the amniotic fluid had gushed forth, not pale and almost clear as it should have been in a pregnancy that was ending right on its due date but stained a dirty brownish green.

Erin had whipped out a stethoscope and checked the foetal heart rate, only to find that it was still dipping seriously with each contraction and not bouncing back up again to well over a hundred beats a minute, as was normal.

And the contractions in this case were unremitting. Sandra was sucking in great heaves of nitrous oxide—laughing gas—in an attempt to take the edge off the pain, but it wasn't working. All it had done had been to loosen her tongue. In the ten-second window between contractions that the gas had opened up, she let fly at full volume with exactly what she was feeling.

'I hate that nurse!'

Erin would have liked to have done the same.

I hate you, Alec Rostrevor!

When she had ducked out of the room a few minutes ago to ask another midwife to summon the resident on call, she'd had no idea, *none,* that this meeting with the past had lain in wait for her. Alec's set, suffering face had told her that for him it had been far less of a shock, but that fate had played him a cruel trick all the same. That he was in Canberra because of her, Erin had no doubt. He wouldn't have chosen to engineer their first meeting in more than two years like this, however.

She had to go back in. She had to face the impossible reality of his presence at a time when they couldn't even begin to talk about it and had to focus every bit of their attention on bringing the imminent birth to a successful conclusion.

The self-control required reminded Erin of the hours of silent, well-masked agony she'd endured at Alec's wedding, when she had partnered his older brother Simon in the bridal party.

She wheeled the more elaborate resuscitation trolley into the delivery room and parked it unobtrusively in the same spot where the innocuous cot had recently stood. Then she caught a stricken look from Ian Taylor. She smiled quickly back at him, trying to reassure him, but it didn't help. He knew something was up. His wife didn't. She was too caught up in her pain, sucking on that gas once again as the contraction climbed inexorably to its height.

Alec's blue eyes skated in Erin's direction, connected for an instant, then sped away again. In the moment of eye contact, she was surprised there hadn't been a crashing sound. Cymbals, or something. A whole symphony orchestra, with emphasis on the percussion section. His face had been masked at the wedding, too. She'd never been able to guess what he'd been thinking that day, how he'd felt. He'd performed his role to perfection—said his vows clearly, made the requisite jokes during his speech.

'Try and push this time, Sandra,' he urged the patient. His dark head was approximately level with her knees as he slid his hand in to massage back one last curled edge of the dilated cervix.

'I can't.'

'Yes, you can.'

Ian Taylor squeezed his wife's hand and echoed Alec's

encouragement. Erin half-expected Sandra to start venting
her pain with a string of profanity in her husband's direction,
but she didn't. Instead, she managed to squeeze his hand back
and give a tiny nod, her grimace still in place. When the
contraction came she took a last desperate lungful of gas then
began to strain downwards with all her might.

She surprised both Erin and Alec—Erin could tell—with
her determination and effectiveness. The baby's head had
moved perceptibly lower into the birth canal by the end of
the contraction.

'You've done this before, Sandra, haven't you?' Alec said,
in the warm yet well-bred drawl to which approximately
ninety-seven per cent of his patients responded so well. His
eyes were focused and clear beneath a level frown.

'Yes,' she gasped. 'Three times. But those were in
America, *where they give you an epidural if you ask for one*!'

Alec gave a short chuckle.

'All right, again, Sandra, with all you've got,' he said.
'Don't waste your time abusing the staff. We're very thick-
skinned and it just won't work.'

She harnessed her strength and pushed again, while her
husband summoned a wilted smile for the doctor's dry, almost self-deprecating humour. Ian still looked anxious, but
he was hiding it well from his wife and giving her everything
he could in the way of support.

She had been dragging on his hand for a good two hours
now, Erin suspected, contorting it, squeezing the circulation
dry, scraping back the skin and drawing blood with her nails,
but he had taken no notice of his own discomfort.

One of the good husbands. Erin loved them and felt for
them. Sometimes they got a bit lost in all the postpartum
excitement, and no one remembered that this was hard for
them, too. She longed to tell him, 'Don't worry about the
Humidicrib, it's just a precaution. Better safe than sorry.' But

there was no opportunity, not without alarming Sandra as well.

Several more pushes brought the head to crowning point, and then, after more pushing and a mighty effort, it appeared, blue and slickly wet, the little face crumpled up. The cord was looped around its neck and Alec freed it carefully. At the same time, he muttered something under his breath which was probably complete nonsense although somehow, as always, he made it sound immensely learned and reassuring.

Erin suctioned out the nose and mouth and wiped the smeared little face clean, swamped in Alec's nearness, aching to touch him despite everything else she felt. His warmth and scent were so familiar, as intoxicating and wonderful as they had been from the beginning. Just the way his shirt moved over his skin was special to her, the way his chin jutted when he was concentrating, the way he sometimes tucked his tongue into his cheek, and the way his hair softly touched the back of his neck. She remembered so clearly how it felt to touch him there, although she'd only done it on one precious occasion.

'OK, that's clear,' he muttered. 'Thanks.'

She stepped back again, breathing hard and feeling momentarily reprieved.

Then Alec attempted to rotate the baby sideways to allow the shoulders to pass through the narrow part of the pelvis. Erin waited for the wonderful moment when the baby slipped free and plopped out like an unusually muscular jellyfish, but this time it didn't happen.

Stuck.

Shoulder dystocia, it was called. Sandra was getting ready to give another one of her Olympic gold medal pushes, fighting the extremely uncomfortable sensation of having a baby poised halfway out.

'Hold it, Sandra, can you?' Alec said calmly. He reached his hand in past the baby's neck to perform the required manoeuvre. His face was focused, eyes narrowed. 'OK, now, give it your very best.'

She did, and so did he. Erin simply held her breath and Ian held Sandra's shoulders. His eyes were closed and his face was squeezed tight and red as if he were the one doing the work.

Then, before it got too frightening, Alec succeeded in freeing the baby's shoulder and he—definitely a he—popped out like a champagne cork on New Year's Eve. Having let out the breath he'd been holding, Alec only just managed to catch the baby before he flew off the end of the table.

'Whoa, caught in the nick of time! It's a boy, Sandra. Congratulations! You did that brilliantly.'

'Yes, we knew it was a boy,' she said in a creaky voice. 'Another darling boy. Oh, he's out, he's out, and it's over.'

She moaned with relief, then lay back with her eyes closed, limp and exhausted and exultant. Meanwhile, the baby was bluer than he should be, and too quiet. Erin began to massage him, then just as she sensed Alec moving closer, ready to intervene, the newborn erupted in a loud cry, and healthy pink began to radiate slowly outwards from his chest.

Erin laid him in his mother's arms, and Sandra cuddled him with her eyes closed so that she wasn't even aware of the oxygen mask Erin slipped over the baby's face for a minute or two until his colour improved more dramatically. He was a big lad, well over four kilograms, at a guess. More than nine pounds on the old scale.

'Does he have a name yet?' Alec asked. He eased the long, pale cord out gently, then told Sandra, 'Push now. Just take it easy but steady. This is the placenta coming.'

'His name is William,' she answered him, then bore down obediently once more.

Alec gently removed a large, healthy-looking and intact placenta, then said—and a stranger would never have known from his face that he knew he was dropping a bombshell in Erin's lap—'Ah, William! That's my son's name.'

His son! His and Kate's.

Well, was it so surprising that they had a child? People had kids. Statistically, even today in an age of rampant single parenthood, married people, especially, had kids.

Married people had kids and then, sometimes, they divorced. Was Alec divorced now? Or was Kate here with him? Surely she couldn't be! Yet it was hard to imagine Alec without gorgeous, confident thirty-two-year-old Kate at his side.

Their child, on the other hand, Erin couldn't imagine at all.

Her world rocked sideways and for a long moment she couldn't breathe. This was too much, wasn't it? Just too many shocks for one routine evening.

'Oops,' Alec said. 'Bit of a gush coming here.'

'Yikes, yes, I can feel it!'

Sandra Taylor was bleeding, a silent swell of red that was heavier than it should have been.

'Your bladder's rather full, isn't it?' he said.

'No idea!'

'Sorry, silly question. You're too swollen and battered to tell. Just relax, if you can, and we'll coax that uterus back into the pelvic cavity where it belongs.'

A few minutes later, everything seemed to be under control once more, and Alec gave a local anaesthetic then stitched up a moderate tear. He wished Mr and Mrs Taylor good luck and told them they had a beautiful, healthy baby. 'Didn't need the Rolls Royce cot after all,' he said, indicating the resus. trolley. Baby William was still snuggled safely in his mother's arms.

Then, after another mute suffering glance at Erin—oh, those blue eyes, as clear as an Australian summer sky—Alec was gone.

Since she still had a considerable amount of work to do

with this patient and her new baby, Erin could no more race from the room to demand an explanation than she could have stood up in front of the congregation, on that late November day in England over two years ago, and objected to his wedding.

Although perhaps that's exactly what I should have done, she had time to muse as she helped Sandra Taylor to the bathroom. *Just to see what he would have said. At least that way I'd have known…*

'I've made up my mind, Erin,' Melusine Rostrevor announced expansively, above the background noise of a crowded London pub. 'I want you for my sister-in-law.'

'Sounds good to me,' Erin agreed easily.

She didn't take the idea too seriously. To be honest, they were both just the teensiest bit tipsy, after enjoying a celebratory cocktail on an empty stomach. It wasn't a very serious sin, when you were single and gainfully employed and twenty-four years old.

Two weeks of holidays lay ahead. Two weeks away from the hospital where she and Mel both worked, and from a London summer which, so far, Australian-bred Erin hardly considered worthy of the name.

Melusine, who was invariably called Mel by everyone except her parents, was going home to her family, while Erin was spending a week in Paris before joining Mel in Tunbridge Wells.

'I'm going to fix you up with my brother,' Mel announced confidently, raising her glass once more. 'Simon needs someone like you. He'll get so pompous, otherwise, by the time he's forty.'

'Wonderful,' Erin agreed.

'No, honestly, he's really very sweet.'

'Great, then. I'd love to be your sister-in-law.'

'Seriously—'

'Seriously, if you don't stop trying so hard to convince me, I'm really going to think there's something wrong with him, Mel.'

The two had been sharing a flat together for three months at this point, and were getting on famously. The flat was Mel's, and Erin suspected that she rented out the spare bedroom more from the need for companionship than to boost her finances, just as she thought of her nursing work not as a Nightingale-style vocation, but as fodder for a future boldly imagined career as a literary sensation. The Rostrevors, Erin had very quickly understood, were better than comfortably situated in life. They were an old, established family, with iron-clad traditions, as Mel had explained a few weeks ago.

'The eldest son goes into the army. The second son goes into the City, and keeps the rest of us in clover with astute advice on investments. Subsequent sons, if any, take their pick from the above two options, and daughters don't count at all. I mean, you can tell that just from our names, can't you? Alec and Simon, such sensible and dependable monikers, versus Melusine, a frivolous choice made from pure whimsy when Mother was under the influence of pain relief. Which is bliss—the fact that daughters don't count, I mean—because otherwise, honestly, the pressure!'

Erin wasn't quite convinced, at this stage, about the pressure. Simon, the eldest, was indeed in the army, and doing so well at it that he must surely belong there. And second son Alec wasn't in the City at all but was a newly trained doctor and was about to start his internship at the same very famous London teaching hospital where Erin and Mel both worked, Erin as a midwife and Mel in Theatre. Could there be all that much pressure?

Mel repeatedly sang Alec's praises and assured Erin that she would love working with him. He had proved a disappointment to his sister in the matter of providing her with a kindred sister-in-law, however. Mel didn't like his fiancée, Kate Gilchrist, at all.

'But, of course, she's gorgeous, and revoltingly suitable, and men are idiots, and what more can I say?' was Mel's unusually acid observation.

So Erin explored Paris with an Australian friend, then travelled to Rostrevor House for her week with Mel.

On the first day there she met Simon, liked him and felt not the remotest spark of either lust or romance. Two days later, she met Alec.

At this point, beneath a soft English summer sky, she fell very quickly, painfully, seriously and secretly in love—with his infectious, almost boyish laugh, his cautious, thoughtful opinions, his erratic flashes of brilliance on the tennis court, his unaccountable streak of wariness, everything about him, actually.

Most of all, perhaps, she fell in love with his body. It was the vessel that contained his soul, the instrument on which the music of his personality was played.

She loved his lean, lightly muscled contours and his English colouring—the fair skin that tanned to a light gold, the eyes like sunshine on a lake, the glints in his hair like the veins of colour in some rich, polished wood. She loved the sober fullness of his lips and the straightness of his nose.

She loved his masculine grace, too, offset by occasional episodes of angular clumsiness—like the time he careered into the tennis net, tried to turn it into a swashbuckling gymnastic manoeuvre and ended up coming down hard on his backside with his tennis racquet between his knees.

Kate was there at the time, and she shrieked then told him lightly not to be such a fool. Didn't move from her position on the opposite side of the court. Alec merely grinned lopsidedly and awarded himself a three out of ten.

Actually, that had probably been the moment...looking back...when the whole thing crystallised in Erin's heart. She had been standing at the picnic table in the little brushwood tennis shelter that looked out onto the Rostrevors' court. She was supposed to have been dispensing tea from a Thermos, but had been distracted by the game. And other things. Such as trying not to look too much at Alec. Or Kate. Wondering why she felt so *awkward* with the woman, when Kate was the embodiment of charm and poised friendliness.

She had seen Alec barrelling towards the net, had seen him flip, had seen the black squares of netting tangle coarsely over his body and heard the bone-crunching thud as he'd landed. Her heart had come into her mouth and boiling water had dripped onto her shoe. She'd put the Thermos down with a crack and had almost run to him, before she'd realised it wasn't her role.

Would have hauled him to his feet, flung her arms around him and chafed that lovely, firm, compact male behind with both hands, then laughed and given him an eight out of ten for imagination and flair and sheer, silly guts.

Meanwhile, Kate had been rolling her eyes prettily and preparing for the next point.

Erin had picked up the Thermos again, said, 'Tea, Simon?' quite calmly and felt her insides drop like a runaway elevator in a New York skyscraper.

I'm in love with him.

Yes, that was definitely the moment.

From then on, the whole thing about becoming a Rostrevor sister-in-law stopped being a bit of a silly game between herself and Mel and became something that too closely resembled the painful plight of Hans Christian Andersen's *The Little Mermaid.*

Mel kept innocently inviting Erin home for the holidays in order to throw her at Simon. Erin didn't dare confess why she wasn't interested in Simon, which created the illusion in Mel that she was actually quite interested indeed. And she didn't want to risk losing Mel's friendship by turning down the invitations, so she kept accepting them.

Endured one perfect, snowy Christmas when various Rostrevor relatives and friends sat around the fire for hours on different occasions, chatting in groups of three or four…or occasionally two…and went for long, cold tramps around the countryside in big coats and hats. Kate didn't make it that year, and Erin was tortured with the dangerous illusion of having Alec to herself.

He didn't do or say a single thing that Kate could have objected to, but he hunted up a spray of fresh eucalyptus leaves for Erin from an eccentric friend's arid-zone green-house. 'I thought you might be homesick.' And when she forgot to take off the magenta and yellow paper party hat which had fallen out of her Christmas cracker at the big mid-day meal, he gently did it for her and didn't make her feel like an idiot because everyone else had taken their hats off an hour ago.

The following Christmas, he wasn't there, which was even worse.

'Spending it with Kate's family, but is hoping to make it here for an afternoon,' Mel reported casually. So Erin spent the whole three days of her stay on tenterhooks, waiting for him to appear. He didn't.

And in London, meanwhile, once he'd finished his intern-ship and had embarked upon further training as an obstetri-cian and gynaecologist, Alec kept showing up on Erin's shift to practise delivering babies. She soon began to feel, every moment that she spent in his presence—especially when Kate was there—as if, like the Little Mermaid, she were walking on knives.

Until almost the very end…

'Leave it until after your shower, Sandra,' Erin suggested to her patient. Mrs Taylor's bladder was still filling, but she was too swollen to be able to empty it yet.

'That's a good idea.' Sandra nodded. 'The shower might help me to relax, or something.'

Her husband was still delightedly holding little William, who had weighed in at a hefty 4325 grams—nearly nine and a half pounds—and passed his physical exam with flying colours after his slightly alarming start. He was now tightly swaddled, as newborns loved to be, and quietly alert.

Moving awkwardly and still hampered by her bleeding, Sandra had her shower and was then able to release her bladder successfully. She put on protective pads and a pretty nightdress, then Erin wheeled her and the baby around to her postpartum room with Ian walking beside them. Another nurse took over at this point, and Erin went back to the birth suite.

Alec sat at the nurses' station, waiting for her.

'I have to fix up the room,' she announced, not sure, herself, whether she was speaking to him or to Leigh Ryan, another nurse taking a paperwork break at the nurses' station.

'Couple of questions, while you're at it,' Alec put in vaguely for Leigh's benefit. He sprang to his feet with the mix of grace and angularity she had always loved and followed her, pulling the wide door of the delivery room shut behind him.

'I'm not going to talk about this now,' she told him defensively at once. 'Leave it till the morning, at least. I have work to do.'

'No,' he answered. 'No!'

He wasn't standing nearly as close to her as he could have done, but she was intensely aware of the placement of his long body all the same. He had his shoulders hunched, his feet were restless on the polished vinyl floor and his lean jaw was stuck out stubbornly. His physical pull on her senses played havoc with her breathing.

'To have it hang fire for the rest of the night?' he went on. 'I couldn't stand it, not knowing if—'

'Not *knowing*?' she whispered harshly, stepping forward. 'How can you dare talk about not knowing, when it was you who left me so totally in the—'

'You left the country!' he retorted.

'Those hours before the wedding were unspeakable!'

'I'd promised Kate—'

'And as for the days after it...'

'When Kate and I got back from our honeymoon, you'd already gone. Mel said you'd picked a fight with her and had done a midnight flit. She was hurt.'

'I—I know. I couldn't stand the thought of staying in touch with her, hearing all your news like bits of trivial chit-chat.'

'You left so quickly.'

'Was I supposed to stay to hear you tell me that Kate was the one you loved after all?'

'That's not what happened. I could have told you—'

'Then what did?' she finished, the words a strident punctuation to their uncompleted sentences, each one ragged with accusation.

He paced and twisted, threw back his head in frustration, making his dark hair flop untidily. He was the kind of man who often found it easier to dam back his emotions or poke fun at them rather than laying them out on the table as Erin was demanding he do now.

She had to give him credit for trying, though, for taking this seriously. A resolute, determined expression had crept onto his face, his blue eyes were steady and clear and he wasn't going to let her retreat to high ground. Despite his clear level of tension, there was a traitorous voice in Erin's head which kept insisting that in this electric state he looked absolutely magnificent. Hair all over the place, hands standing out from his sides, half-clenched into fists, shirtsleeves absently pushed up to reveal smoothly muscled forearms.

'I thought you might have guessed by now,' he said to her slowly. The atmosphere in the room suddenly stilled. 'Kate was pregnant.'

Erin didn't know how many times she had relived that magic day in late November nearly two and a half years ago when he'd told her, at last, how he felt.

They'd left the hospital together in the morning darkness after a busy, difficult night. 'I'll run you home,' he'd said easily, and she'd accepted because she'd kept trying to behave 'normally' with him—the way she'd felt she'd have behaved if this had been just any plain old, insignificant, vaguely friendly brother of Mel's.

They weren't so very far apart in age. He was just three years older—twenty-nine at this point—and because he hadn't started medicine straight out of school, he had still been at the very beginning of his career. He wasn't someone she'd have found intimidating in other circumstances, since she had three older brothers of her own.

Then he'd suggested rather woodenly that they stop somewhere for coffee and croissants, and she had accepted that, too, thinking that, after all, she was almost getting used to this walking-on-knives feeling. She had been doing it for over two years by this time, and Alec and Kate's much-postponed-and-anguished-over wedding was just three days away.

'I have to tell you, something very difficult and strange has happened, Erin.'

He didn't lead up to the subject with a lot of preamble. They were still waiting to receive their order. His words were effortful, breaking free like a pressure cooker with a leaky valve.

'Has it?' she said brightly, too busy watching the way his fine fingers played with the sugar dispenser to properly take in what he'd said.

'Yes. I've discovered that I'm terribly in love with you.'

Talk about appetite suppressants! She couldn't eat a thing, or take more than a sip or two of her coffee. He had made the abrupt confession with an expression of agony, as if he didn't dare to begin to hope that what he felt might be reciprocated, and as if it had cost him hugely to reach this point of declaration at all.

Had she said anything remotely coherent in reply? She couldn't remember. Maybe she'd simply looked at him. All she knew was that suddenly they were kissing hungrily across the café tabletop, hands joined, mouths hot and insatiable, drinking each other in, words garbled and fragmentary.

'I never—I thought— But Kate—' she blurted eventually.

'I've known for ages,' he said, his voice a painful creak. 'In my heart, anyway. I can see it now. Not my head, though.' He pressed his hands against his temples. His eyes were narrowed. 'My head only caught up about two days ago. I was too…I don't know…afraid?'

'You, Alec?' she challenged him huskily. 'Afraid? I didn't think you knew how to be afraid.'

'No, not that,' he agreed. 'Blocked, somehow. Well, sick about disappointing my parents. Again. I told you about that, didn't I?'

'Yes, the Christmas before last, by the fire, when it was snowing and everyone else was sleeping off the turkey.'

She still remembered that scene in great detail, too. He had simply stared into the fire and poured out his life story in one long, erratic narrative, and she'd discovered that Mel hadn't been exaggerating when she'd spoken about pressure. Attendance at a certain well-known public school, where he hadn't had quite the right brash sort of temperament to be popular, a year in the City dealing with money matters in which he hadn't been remotely interested, pressure and unhappiness building to breaking point, followed by a sudden, emotional rebellion against becoming a financier that had

earned total yet very vocal repudiation by Mr and Mrs
Rostrevor for more than a year.

He had spent six months trying to make it as a stand-up
comedian. Failed at it dismally. 'Not funny, unfortunately.'
Tried cabinet-making. 'Too wooden. The cabinets, that is.
Not me.' She'd sensed that he hadn't been able to joke about
it like this at the time, and that the jokes, even years later,
were a little forced.

Then he discovered a vocation for medicine like a flash of
lightning and didn't look back. Loved it. Reconciled in a
tenuous way with his parents and tried to please them by
continuing to play the stock market.

At the ripe old age of twenty-two, he ended up losing
about seventy thousand pounds inherited from a great-uncle.
'And honestly couldn't care less. Compared with losing a
patient—which I did, in tragic circumstances, at around the
same time—it just didn't rate.'

It wasn't until he began to specialise in obstetrics that his
parents gave their grudging approval of his career choice,
since there was sufficient status attached. By that time, too,
he'd announced his engagement to Kate Gilchrist, whom they
adored. Why wouldn't they? Most people did. She was
charming to everyone, she came from an extremely good
family, she was poised on the brink of a successful acting
career, and she was very, very beautiful.

'Lord, I was a fool!' Alec muttered, pressing Erin's hands
to his lips across the café table. 'That first summer, and then
at Christmas and ever since. Just kept thinking you were that
very nice, sunny colonial friend of Mel's with the wonderful
smile and sparkling eyes.'

'Colonial? Arrogant pom!'

'I was. You're quite right. But I've seen sense.'

More kisses. Laughter. His face changed, relaxed, to a re-
markable degree in just ten minutes. His eyes blazed, his
smile was incredible. She still remembered how his mood

had surrounded her, drawn her in, made her almost drunk with happiness.

'What on earth are we going to do?'

The ringing confidence of her question to him that day haunted her now. Her use of 'we'. Her certainty that they could 'do' something. The way she'd run her fingers lightly, possessively, across the back of his hand as she'd spoken.

'I'll tell Kate tomorrow,' he'd said. 'She only gets back then. This ghastly film she's been working on. Hell, I should have told her three weeks ago that something was wrong, but when she bought those first-class tickets as a surprise, for us to meet up in Rome...' He had shaken his head. 'I should have trusted it. My intuition about you, I mean. But I kept thinking, is this the stand-up-comedy thing all over again?'

'You were nineteen then. It's more than ten years ago.'

'No, but I'm talking about that same sense of panicky flight. The dam inside you bursts. You're swept along. Do you trust it or not? You know what you're rejecting. You know something is horribly wrong with your life, but your judgement isn't clear. You don't know if the alternative that you've found is just running away, just the rock that those flood-waters of feeling have chanced to wash you up against. I didn't trust what my heart was starting to tell me about you, so I did my best in Rome with Kate and kidded myself that we'd had a good time.'

'Do you trust your intuition now?'

'Yes. Yes, I do.' A melting grin. 'Absolutely.'

They went back to her flat. Mel was at work. They said all sorts of things to each other, made crazy plans, almost slept together. Not quite, thank goodness. They shared the same sense of honour about that, and reined in a passionate spate of exultation and discovery that was so close to un-stoppable it actually *hurt* to put on the brakes.

She remembered how his hands had hovered at her breasts, brushing the aching peaks through the fine lace and net of her bra, before he'd dropped them to his sides with a groan. She remembered her own hands splaying against the back of his head, pulling him down to meet her swollen, trembling mouth for one last kiss...two last kisses...three...

Finally, he'd had to press the back of his hand against his mouth and take a step backwards, while she had fallen to the couch, clutching a cushion to her chest to hide the way her nipples had hardened. She could still feel, in her memory, the cool, slippery fabric on her tingling skin.

'Not until I tell her,' he said, the words almost incomprehensible through the hand that was still pressed against his mouth. 'Not until I call off the wedding.' He dropped his hand at last and faced her with eyes and cheeks blazing. 'Don't say anything to Mel, will you? Or Simon. *Anyone*!'

'Of course I won't.'

'It has to come from me.' He dragged in a heaving breath. 'I couldn't have them hating you, and I want to leave it to Kate to decide how we put it. That's only fair. If she wants to tell people that it was her decision.'

So Erin waited. Patiently. In agony. Those knives in her feet again! Then not patiently any more but in a cold sweat of panic and need and blind faith. It was Friday and she still hadn't heard a word from him. Mel was frothing with excitement, chattering extravagantly about their bridesmaids' dresses, their flowers and their hair. They went down on the train on Friday evening, and once more, under Alec's parents' roof, Erin waited, imprisoned behind iron bands of control.

Nothing.

She didn't see Alec. He was coming down on Saturday morning, after working late the night before, and by the time he arrived, Mel and Erin had already gone over to Kate's parents' house to help her dress, along with Kate's younger sister Sarah and friend Anna, who were the other bridesmaids.

It wasn't until the time came to leave for the picture-perfect church that Erin finally accepted the reality that Alec wasn't coming. He wasn't going to talk to Kate—who looked tall, slim and utterly radiant in cream silk, with her rich pile of russet hair and chocolate brown eyes. He wasn't going to cancel the wedding. He was going to go through with it, and no one who looked at the endearingly nervous and stunningly lovely thirty-year-old bride would have needed to ask why.

Erin felt like a cheap, young, blonde, colonial upstart, without even the skerrick of a 'wonderful' smile or 'sparkling' eyes. She was angry and foolish and wounded to the core. Had Alec been using her? Had he intended a last fling with her, before the chains of wedlock bound him, then belatedly got brought up short by his conscience? Had he just manufactured all that stuff about newly realised love?

At least Mel hadn't guessed. Jolly, pompous, didn't-know-how-to-talk-to-girls Simon hadn't guessed. Alec's coolly civilised parents hadn't guessed. *No one* had guessed.

And Alec hadn't said a word. Until now.

'Kate told me about the baby that Thursday, two days before the wedding,' Alec explained.

He slid the linen bin six inches out from the wall with his foot. Erin bundled the soiled sheets in her arms and dumped them into it. They were both trying to pretend that they were doing something useful.

'So you went through with it,' she said.

'I was gobsmacked. So was she. It must have happened those two days in Rome, when I…hated making love to her, if you want the truth. She was just getting people to take notice of her as an actress at last, after years of work. Didn't want a baby. Maybe not ever, she said, and certainly not then. She was panicking about it. Kept talking about a termination.'

'And calling off the—?' she began, but she knew he didn't mean that.

'No, *not* calling off the wedding. Just terminating the pregnancy.' He pressed his palms hard against his eyes. 'I couldn't understand that. When she still claimed to love me. And I couldn't begin to contemplate it. To stand by and... To let her—'

'You don't have to explain that part,' Erin said quickly. 'I understand.'

'Do you?' He looked relieved, almost disbelieving.

'We feel the same about things like that, don't we? There was an incident at the hospital once. We talked about it.'

He nodded. 'In the lift. I remember. Only took half a minute to cover the subject. That was one of the things I first noticed about you—that your priorities were so warm and human and simple.' He let out a sigh. 'Kate...is ruled by different passions, I found.'

'Tell me, Alec.'

'We talked and talked. It went on for hours, round and round in circles. She finally agreed to go through with the pregnancy as long as I promised to go ahead with the wedding and do whatever was necessary to stop it getting in the way of her career. I wanted to tell you, but didn't trust that if we talked I'd still be able to go through with it. And Kate wanted me to promise not to say one word to anyone about her being pregnant until we got back from the Caribbean. You see, she didn't want to spoil her image, spoil the photogenic perfection of the wedding, in anyone's eyes.'

'It certainly was perfect,' Erin agreed. 'You even got good weather. In November! And I looked at you in that dashing grey morning suit, and her so stunningly beautiful, with her flawless English skin and not a hair or a stroke of make-up out of place.'

'Beautiful? Yes, but not like you. She doesn't shine like you do...'

Erin ignored him. 'Even the church, for heaven's sake, Gothic, or whatever it was, glowing golden in the slanting autumn sunlight, the Gilchrist family seat of worship since the Battle of Something-or-other. Since Boadicea and the building of Stonehenge, probably. And it just seemed so painfully obvious that I didn't fit anywhere in that picture. You didn't even look at me,' she remembered. 'You kissed me on the cheek.'

She could almost feel the cold, dry touch of his lips, and the perfunctory squeeze of his hands on her upper arms, clad in apricot silk.

'I had to kiss you,' he said simply. 'It was expected.'

'But you didn't look at me.'

'I couldn't.'

'And it seemed insane that I'd thought even for a moment that we could fit into each other's lives.'

'I'm here now, aren't I?' he pointed out.

She buried her face in her hands. 'Don't do this!'

'Do what?'

'Say it like that. As if suddenly, after more than two years, it's simple again, like it was that day when we had coffee and you told me. It can't ever be that simple. Ever. You must be able to see that. And I have work to do. There are two patients coming in. Go and get some sleep in the on-call room.'

'And we'll talk about it in the morning.'

'If you think there's anything more to say.'

'Believe me, Erin Gray, there's a hell of a lot more to say!'

His eyes sparked hot and blue. There was an uncompromising determination in him that she'd only ever seen before in the context of his work, and an exultant confidence that she'd only seen once before, too. The day he'd first told her he loved her.

She didn't answer him, but she knew quite well this wasn't over. How could it be, when she'd wanted him, needed him and loved him for more than four years?

CHAPTER TWO

IT WAS morning when Erin left the hospital.

Savoury breakfast smells were wafting through the building, and there was the sound of clunking trolleys and rattling cutlery echoing along corridors. The doctors' car park had begun to fill, and there was a delivery truck exceeding the cautious speed limit on a service road.

The March sunlight was strengthening, spearing golden through the eucalyptus and wattle trees that formed a thick swathe of dry, scrubby bushland around Black Mountain Hospital. It would be pleasantly warm today, once the sun rose higher, but at the moment it was still crisp and cool, one of those bright, clear Canberra autumn mornings that Erin had grown up with and loved.

Home beckoned—the compact two-bedroomed town house with a small walled garden which Erin rented. The place was ten minutes' drive from here, and just five minutes walk along quiet suburban streets from her brother Gordon's house, where he lived with his wife Rachel and their little boy, two-year-old Archie.

Erin would make herself breakfast, something hot and substantial, then she would go to bed, sleep till about three and then and *only* then would she think about—

Alec. Her pulses leaped, and something throbbed deep inside her.

He was leaning against a 'No Standing' sign with his back to her and the collar of his silvery grey shirt open. His head was tilted back, letting the golden sun soak into his face and neck. It was a pose that was absorbed and unselfconscious, totally relaxed and almost worshipful. As soon as he heard

27

footsteps approaching, however, he opened his eyes, straightened and checked who was coming and, yes, obviously he had been waiting for her.

He smiled. It crinkled up the skin around his brilliant blue eyes.

'The sun is gorgeous,' he said. 'Unbelievable.' It caught at his hair and brought out glints of red and dark gold in the rich brown.

'I know,' Erin said, deliberately short. 'Be careful. Your skin will age at twice the speed.'

'Good. I have screaming women in labour, all the time, accusing me of being too young to deliver their babies.'

She didn't laugh, and there was a silence.

He pressed on. 'Coming for coffee and croissants, then?'

He said it so lightly, as if it meant nothing, was just a casual offer, but she knew he'd said it deliberately, and it took both of them right back to that other, much darker morning more than two years ago.

'No,' she answered him.

'I'm hoping that's just your opening bid.'

His voice was low and sincere, but with a lick of humour around the edges. There was an indefinable glow inside him, as if he had arrived at some secret enlightenment he'd been striving for all his life. It was electric, filled him with energy and spilled over into Erin herself.

But it came out as anger.

'And that I'm going to drop into your outstretched hand like a ripe plum?' she demanded. 'I'm *not*, Alec! I'm not ripe. I'm green and hard and I'm *not dropping*!'

The last word had a sob attached. She pushed past him, her rubber-soled shoes thumping at a rapid rhythm on the cement walkway.

'Erin... Erin!'

He was following her, loping to keep up with her angry pace. She quickened her steps almost to a run, reached her little red car, unlocked it clumsily, opened the door and turned to stand there, glaring at him. The door acted as a barrier, with her forearm resting along the top of the cold metal.

For a long moment they faced each other in angry silence, while she fought the pull between them, then he said huskily, 'Look, doesn't it mean something to you that I'm here? Doesn't that tell you something? Not here on a flying two week visit either, but here to live and to work. Because of you, Erin. Purely to prove to you that Kate was the mistake and you're the reality.'

She lifted her chin. 'I have questions about that.'

'I know you do. So ask them. Let's go somewhere and talk.'

'My place. I'm not having this out in public.'

'Your place. Perfect.'

'And when I tell you to leave, you'll leave?'

'I'll leave,' he promised. 'When you tell me.'

'Do you have a car here?'

'I have everything here. I have a whole life. I'm serious about this, Erin, more serious than I can express. And I've been here almost two weeks.'

It was a conspiracy, with covert operatives working in two hemispheres.

Erin had realised this by the time she reached home. Alec's green Volvo was still visible in the rear-view mirror behind her. She glared at it as she swung the wheel and pulled into her short driveway, but she wasn't thinking of Alec at the moment, she was thinking of two interfering sisters, her own sister Caitlin and Alec's sister Mel.

They had to be involved in this. Possibly even her sister-in-law Rachel was, too, and the way she felt at the moment, they were all three of them now permanently off her Christmas card list.

Why, though?

Wasn't this the happy-ever-after that women dreamed of? A gorgeous, successful, intelligent, wonderful man, a man who set her pulses racing, made her laugh, made her hands and mouth ache to touch him and drained the strength from her limbs, had come halfway around the world to be with her and to declare his love. What more could she ask for?

I'd have believed it two years ago, she knew. We'd have raced off to bed in the first minute, and I'd have thought all my troubles were over. But I'm older now...

'Come in,' she told him, after he'd parked behind her. 'I'm hungry. Mind if I make a huge breakfast?'

'Night shift appetite? Sounds good.'

'Eggs and bacon and coffee and juice?'

'Throw in toast and a grilled tomato or two and I'm yours. I *am* yours, by the way, Erin,' he added softly. 'All yours.'

She ignored him. Went to her tidy, eccentrically decorated room instead, changed out of her subtly patterned blue uniform tunic and tailored navy trousers and into dark olive cargo pants and a thin, long-sleeved cream knit top. Then she came back to the bright but rather poky kitchen, where he sat at her small, round table. He was staring at yesterday's newspaper, but she wasn't convinced he was reading it.

She clattered about violently, breaking eggs, disembowelling oranges, cleaving tomatoes with a scalpel-sharp knife. He didn't offer to help, for which she was grateful.

None of that cosy domesticity, thanks! The modern alpha male was getting just a little too good at that particular trick, worming his way into a woman's heart with the quick toss of an omelette in a pan, sleeves rolled up and lazy grin in place.

Domesticity... The thought led to images of Alec's son.

'Where's William?' she asked suddenly, over the sound of bacon sizzling.

'At home,' he said.

'In London,' she clarified, 'with Kate?'

'With Kate?' he echoed, startled. 'No! Heavens, no, Erin! He's not with Kate. She didn't want him in the end. He's with me.'

She turned from the stove. 'You see, that's *exactly* why this isn't simple!' she exclaimed hotly, then burst into tears.

The eggs were ruined, of course. They salvaged the bacon, but that was later.

Alec crossed to her at once and took her into his arms. She wanted to fight him, but it was too hard. She had wanted him like this for too long. The scent of him, the shape of him. Shoulders shuddering, she wiped her tear-dampened face against the shoulder of his silver-grey shirt, heard the low, soothing sounds he made and felt his lips press the top of her head.

He cradled her against the warmth of his chest, supported her with his strength and didn't say anything coherent, just let her cry until she was ready to stop. She tried to do this too soon, because she wanted to talk, but the words only came out like jerky, uncontrolled squeaks.

'Wait,' he soothed. 'Wait, Erin.'

He kissed her a little, coaxingly—touching her mouth with his, brushing her lips softly with sensation and warmth. She felt a tiny puff of coolness there from his breath, and caught the taste of fresh orange juice. She fought the need to respond, to sink against him and part her lips and surrender, even while her body was still shaking as she struggled against her tears. His hands wandered as if savouring her, and each place they touched caught fire. She felt the heavy heat of physical need building low down inside her.

'We're in no hurry,' he said.

This caught her interest, and after a moment she controlled herself enough to say, 'Aren't we? Don't you have to get home to him?'

'I'd like to, yes, for a quick lunch, before the clinic I have at two.'

'Clinic. You have a clinic?' She made it into an accusation, as if him having a clinic was part of Caitlin's and Mel's machinations. 'This'll be, what, your second day on the job, and already you have a clinic?'

'Yes, you see, I'm replacing someone who had to leave suddenly, a week earlier than planned,' he explained patiently. His hands curved around the tops of her thighs. Their legs were pressed hard against each other like tree trunks that had grown together with time. 'That's why we met up the way we did, last night, instead of me phoning you within the next couple of days, as I'd planned to do. They threw me in at the deep end. Don't think that I wanted us to connect out of the blue at work like that, Erin. Hell, of course I didn't! I wanted to get William settled in, get the practical things organised and then contact you.'

She nodded, convinced, then brushed all this aside. 'I want to talk about William.'

'He has a nanny, who lives in when I'm on call,' Alec said, still as patient and straightforward as before. 'I got her through an agency, and she seems very good. Takes him to play-group twice a week. Makes healthy meals that he likes. Happy to keep flexible hours and change her plans at short notice.'

'Seems good?'

'*Is,*' he corrected himself. 'I tend to get too anxious about some things in this fatherhood game. Erin, I'm not finding single parenthood easy.'

'Does anyone?'

'I need to build my career, finish my training, yet a child's needs are huge. I tell myself it's normal to second-guess my choices and decisions about William several times a week!'

'And yet you left England, where you had all that support,' she challenged him.

'Ha! Support? Who in England is speaking to me at the moment? Not my parents. Certainly not Kate's. They all blame me for the divorce.'

'And, of course, you let them do it,' she guessed, knowing his sense of honour. 'You probably encourage it, in fact.'

He shrugged, didn't deny it. 'They're right to blame me, aren't they?'

'Does Kate think so? Who does she blame? Not herself.'

'Kate is dignified about the whole thing. Analytical, on some occasions. Given to displays of quite charismatic emotion on others. She blames many factors, but mostly it's William.'

'Oh. A one-year-old. Of course.'

He laughed raggedly. 'I don't really need to explain to you why we're divorced now, do I?'

She didn't answer. Didn't want to incriminate herself by admitting the degree to which they instinctively agreed about things. Didn't want to confess openly to what she felt about Kate, because it was murky, complicated. And possibly...*probably*...irrelevant.

'Anyway,' he went on, 'Simon is overseas with a UN peace-keeping force. Mel's the only one who has an inkling of what went on between Kate and me.'

'Ah, yes, Mel,' she said darkly. 'I was coming to Mel. She interfered, didn't she?'

Again, he leapt ahead several steps in the conversation. 'No, Mel is only the accessory after the fact. You never gave her your address here, remember? Caitlin, your sister, is the real instigator.'

'I knew it! She got in touch with you.'

'With Mel. Phoned her at the flat.'

'Mel...'

'Who had guessed most of it, and then wormed the rest out of me.'

'Mel's good at that.'

'She didn't worm it out of you. She hadn't guessed, at all, how you felt until after you fled the country.'

'Because I already knew how good at worming she was, so I was on my guard.'

'She's forgiven you for the fight you staged, by the way. And she and Caitlin were the ones who persuaded me not to contact you beforehand. Kept telling me to wait! Wait!'

'Caitlin knows about William, then?'

'Yes, Mel thought it was…uh…rather relevant.'

'Nice! Oh, this is *nice*!' She rolled her tear-reddened eyes and started to cry once more, gripping two fistfuls of his grey shirtsleeves without even thinking about it.

'Don't make me kiss you again, Erin,' he threatened softly, tightening his hold around her. 'It would be so incredibly easy to do it, and mean it, and just keep going. For a long time. But don't.'

She could feel all of him now. Thighs, stomach, chest, arms. Each part warm and hard, familiar and yet still new. They made her melt from core to skin.

'No? It's what you want, isn't it? So why not?' she demanded, not knowing what she was saying any more. She closed her eyes and pressed her lips together.

'Because, damn it, I'm trying to play this as straight and fair as I can. I've come out here with William. I'm offering you my life, and I've burned my bridges. That felt… fabulous, actually.' She could see that, *feel* it, to be strictly accurate, sense it in the exultant energy that still radiated from him. 'Meet me halfway, like Caitlin told me you would if I showed you I was serious.'

'What does Caitlin know about any of this?' she retorted, stiffening and pushing her palms hard against his chest.

He let her go, and she stepped back, taking the ruined eggs off the stove before they burst into flames. She stood there holding the overheated handle of the pan, wrapped in a tea-towel.

He said, suddenly bleak, his face immediately closing up, 'So this is all a mistake, then? You don't love me. I've come all this way. I want you and need you so much. Have done for two years and more. And you're turning me away.'

What?

'Oh, no! No, of course I love you!' she answered help-lessly, half laughing and half in tears. '*Of course* I love you, Alec Rostrevor!'

She dropped the frying pan into the sink, where it hissed with steam and juddered against the wet stainless steel.

'There!' she went on wildly. 'You've made me say it.'

She put her hands on her hips and glared at him. He hadn't relaxed yet. He looked startled, eyes hot with blue fire, lips parted a little, still wary and waiting.

And gorgeous, with his shirt having somehow two buttons undone now, and his hair a dark, glinting mess.

'So are you happy?' she continued. 'Are you? I love you still, as much as ever, and probably more, when I haven't seen you in more than two years, when I last saw you at your own wedding, when I haven't even met your child yet, and when I thought till last night that I was never going to see you again. But if you think that solves everything, then you're so wrong! So damned, *bloody* wrong, and there's a piece of colonial straight-talking for you!'

'Glad we got that sorted out, then,' he said somewhat help-lessly.

'Sorted out? *Sorted out*?'

She wanted to yell at him that nothing had been sorted out at all, but the words wouldn't come because at heart he was right. It had been sorted out. They loved each other. One small life-raft of simplicity to cling to in a storm-tossed sea of complex issues. William, for example. And Kate.

'OK, not quite sorted out, but...' Alec spread his hands, didn't finish.

He sat down at the table with some care, as if he were

afraid Erin might have mined the seat of the chair with fire-
crackers. The fact that he was still here surprised her. She'd
already given him more than one cue to storm out in disgust.
But she remembered that he wasn't a man who let go of
things lightly. Even when he should.

Perhaps she should take the initiative instead, and fling him
out?

But then he gave her an upside-down smile and under-
mined this intention completely by saying, 'Can I...er...have
my breakfast now, then?'

'If you're prepared to wait while I have another go at the
eggs,' she retorted.

'Perhaps I could tackle them this time?'

Erin decided that she might as well make her capitulation
complete.

'Sure,' she answered, flinging her hands in the air. 'Go
ahead. Tuck a teatowel into the back pocket of your pants.
Roll up your sleeves. Wield the egg flipper like a swordsman
in a fencing contest. Impress me with your cooking, and we'll
take it from there.'

'I thought tourism would probably be the best bet,' Erin said
to Alec on the phone.

'Not the War Memorial and the National Gallery and all
that? Not with a nineteen-month-old!' he answered deci-
sively.

'No, of course not.' She was nervous, and knew it showed
in her voice, which tended to crack or go husky by turns
when she felt ill at ease.

This was Friday night, four days after their first fraught
meeting. He had managed to phone her every day for a short
snatch of conversation, and they'd crossed paths twice at
work, but each time only briefly. Hardly long enough to warrant her aching for him for the rest of the day, but she'd
ached anyway.

Both of them were taking it carefully. After the drama of those first hours together, there was now a lull. Deceptive, Erin knew. She'd admitted that she loved him. Yelled it, really. It had been more like an accusation than a declaration. And she didn't need him to say that he loved her. When a man uprooted his life and that of his child to come halfway around the world to find you, you'd be a fool if you questioned the existence of his love.

But love was only the beginning sometimes. She knew it. She'd seen it. Look at her sister Caitlin and her husband Angus, clinging white-knuckled to their marriage as if it were the safety bar on a roller-coaster through the pain of Caitlin's doubtful fertility.

Caitlin had had an ectopic pregnancy and lost an ovary and a Fallopian tube two years ago after severe scarring caused by an unsuspected chlamydial infection contracted from her former fiancé, Scott. Several months ago she had finally achieved a second pregnancy via the remaining ovary and tube. She'd ecstatically announced it to everyone in a series of bubbly, tearful phone calls, only to then lose the baby less than a week later in one of those inexplicable early miscarriages that just had to be accepted.

Now she and Angus had each taken a deep breath and were trying again to conceive. Not talking about it this time, neither their fears nor their hopes. Third time lucky? They still seemed strong together, despite what they were going through. Stronger, in fact, than when they had first married in a white heat of new love.

But not all couples managed that. Some marriages split apart, like a wooden boat splintering on a concealed rock, when they hit unexpected trouble.

Erin and Alec weren't the only two people in this particular landscape of feelings. Most importantly, there was William, whom Erin wanted to meet in the best possible circumstances as soon as she could. And lurking in the background, half a world away but alive and complex and real, was beautiful, self-absorbed, strong-willed Kate.

'I meant Paddy's River and Tidbinbilla Nature Reserve,' Erin explained to Alec. 'I know a great spot where William can dabble in the water, and I thought he might be old enough to be interested in emus and koalas and kangaroos. You, too, for that matter. We could take sausages and lamb chops and have an Aussie barbecue on the public gas grills.'

'Sorry,' he said. 'I should have known you wouldn't have suggested swanning around an art gallery with a frustrated toddler on a beautiful autumn day.'

Don't compare me with Kate, she almost said. Even when you're telling me I come out ahead.

Then she thought better of it. After all, he hadn't actually mentioned Kate by name. Maybe the comparison was only in her own head, and he wasn't thinking of his ex-wife at all.

Lord, am I jealous of Kate?

Yes. So early in the game, yes! Perhaps I always have been. And perhaps I wouldn't be human if I wasn't. But it's the last thing I want Alec to suspect.

'We'll take my car, because I have the car seat,' he suggested, and that made sense.

'Since you're providing the transport, I'll do the food,' she answered lightly, and they ended the conversation a few minutes later, with the unacknowledged understanding between them that tomorrow was a hugely important test.

She didn't sleep.

Well, she must have slept a bit, because at some point during the night she did find the opportunity for a vivid nightmare in which Alec entrusted her with William and she somehow concluded that to leave him strapped alone in his car seat on the railway platform at Sevenoaks was the most appropriate form of child-care while she went up to a strange, dream version of London for the day.

In the nightmare, she was stranded on the fast-moving train when realisation dawned… On the platform? All by himself? Was I insane? And she couldn't get the train to stop so she could go back for him before a kidnapping ensued.

She woke up panting and in a cold sweat, convinced that it was a telling indicator of her future capability as a step-parent, and, since it was three o'clock in the morning, she worried about it in the dark for the next two hours.

In the morning, things were slightly more in perspective, but all the same she wasn't at all happy with what she saw in the mirror.

Blonde. Frivolous shoulder-length Aussie blonde, that turned to frizz in humid weather, although on a day like today it rippled quite nicely. Lean, brown limbs. High, tanned fore-head, some little freckles on her nose, summer-blue eyes, lips whose shape she had never liked. Smooth, wide, symmetrical and softly pink, yes, but too *flat* somehow. Weren't they? Female friends laughed when she said this, but Erin remained unconvinced.

Her smile wasn't bad, however. Alec had said it was one of the first things he'd noticed about her. Her dazzling, won-derful smile and sparkling eyes. She tried it in the mirror. Ouch! Cheesy in the extreme, as false as a game-show host, because she was so nervous.

What if he takes one look at me and cries?

Not Alec, of course, but William. Because if he didn't like her, it would definitely matter.

So she found herself dressing for William instead of for Alec. Never mind dressing for herself! She came a distant third today. Fourth, if you counted fashion-conscious, elegant Kate. So she dressed for William. Brightly patterned calf-length pants and an orange cotton blouse. Big straw hat with gumnuts on it. Open-toed sandals so she could paddle easily in Paddy's River, despite the possibility of snakes at

Tidbinbilla, which dictated closed-in shoes and socks as the better choice.

She ate a small tub of yoghurt for breakfast, rushed out to the supermarket to pick up picnic supplies and was ready very, very early.

Alec pulled into the driveway when she was in the kitchen checking the clock for the twelfth time, and she came through into the living room in time to see a taut, jeans-clad male backside sticking out through the open rear door of the vehicle as he unstrapped William from his car seat.

The sight opened up a hollow pit of need deep in her stomach. She wanted to tiptoe up behind him, say something raunchy and claim him with her hands, before he turned hungrily into her embrace. Instead, she forced herself to stay put.

'Hi,' he said a minute later, at the door. 'I didn't want to introduce you in the car so I brought him in.'

'Hello, William,' she managed, huskiness fully in place.

Safe in his daddy's arms, he looked at her unsmilingly, a little semi-blond, fair-skinned, brown-eyed angel in navy corduroy pants and a matching turtleneck, with exactly three little curls nestling soft and fine at the back of his head.

'Say hello to Erin, William,' Alec encouraged, watching his son with a soft face. The pose emphasised the lean length of his neck.

'Huwo,' William said.

'Can I hold you, William?'

'Are you sure?' Alec came in doubtfully.

'Of course. I have nephews and nieces. Don't think my arms will drop off.' Sounded more confident than she felt, to be honest.

Alec gave an upside-down smile, a little sheepish about his moment of scepticism. 'OK, then.'

He bundled the little boy across to her, then stood watching, hands bracketed loosely on his hips and elbows sticking out. William hadn't smiled. But he wasn't crying, and that was something. Then, still staring intently into her face, he reached out his little fingers and stuck them solemnly into her mouth to explore.

She laughed, and so did William and Alec, and she suddenly knew that this part of it, at least, was going to be all right. Toddlers were simple in their affections and had blessedly short memories. He didn't know that she was hoping to replace Kate in Alec's life.

He would soon forget about Kate entirely, in fact, and this would have been heart-breaking if Kate had cared. Apparently she didn't, which left plenty of room for Erin. Not his mother, but the next best thing.

Gently, she took his hand out of her mouth and popped him down on the floor. Alec seemed quietly pleased about the little moment between Erin and his son. They both watched as William toddled off to examine the group of three-dimensional wooden puzzles she kept on her coffee-table and started making them into a tower.

'Can I take anything to the car?' Alec offered.

'Yes, there are a couple of boxes in the kitchen.'

'Right.' He nodded, then his lips shut firmly.

He hadn't kissed her, and she didn't want him to. They were being very circumspect on that point so far, very cautious. Erin was glad about this. Not that it was easy. Right at this moment, she could have closed her eyes and predicted the exact moment when he came back into the room, purely on the strength of the way her skin prickled and tightened, and all her senses stirred, trembled and leapt to life.

At some point, there was going to be a conflagration, but she had sense enough to know that they both needed to hold back until more had been said. The last thing she wanted was to let sex…passionate, hungry, love-filled sex…cloud her judgement.

Or his.

They set off a few minutes later, delayed slightly by

William kicking and screaming as he was removed from his play. Erin considered this a perfectly reasonable response on his part. After all, he had no idea that there were better things than puzzle towers still to come. So she was unperturbed by the outburst, and it soon subsided.

In the car, directing Alec over Coppins Crossing and out along the Cotter Road through commercial pine forests and then open, hilly sheep country, she had questions. Didn't quite know how to ask them. Alec made it easy.

He turned his attention from the road just long enough to sweep her with a heated sideways glance that sent coils of need looping through her stomach, and drawled, 'Come on. This is as good a time as any, isn't it? Don't you want to hear about the divorce?'

'Before that. The birth, first.' She shifted sideways and watched him.

'The divorce *was* before the birth,' he said. 'Or, at least, we were good and separated by then.'

'Oh, Alec!'

'How could it ever have worked? How?' He raked his fingers through his hair. 'It was a disaster from the beginning—from the moment she knew she was pregnant—and would have been even if it hadn't been for you…'

'Does she know about me?' she asked, nervous about it.

'She does now, but only since I decided to make the move here.'

'OK,' she said cautiously.

'As soon as there was the question of a baby, the differences between us were just impossible to ignore. The way we each envisaged our lives. The priorities we placed on things. She felt I'd blackmailed her into opting against a termination.'

'*Blackmailed?*'

'The emotional kind. She was probably right.'

'*You* were right!'

'She said she loved me but had wanted to build up our respective professional lives first, not get saddled with responsibilities and stretch marks and nappies. She wanted to travel, and she had her sights set on more film roles after her successes with theatre. We had some horrible fights. I couldn't understand how she could claim to love me while coolly discussing her regret at not...well, at not having simply gone out and got rid of our child.' He broke off. 'Thank goodness he's not old enough to understand any of this!'

She turned in the passenger seat. 'He's asleep, actually.'

'Is he? Good.'

Erin stayed twisted around watching the child for a few moments. His plump, butter-soft cheek had sunk onto his little shoulder. His lips were pouty like berries, and his lashes, like his father's, were long and thick and dark below the creamiest lids she'd ever seen. Her nephew Archie was a handsome child, but this little boy was gorgeous.

'Anyway...' Alec sighed and blew through his lips. Once again he wiped his fingers back through his dark brown hair and scratched a neck that was already lightly tanned by the Australian sun. 'She didn't look after herself as well as I wanted her to during the pregnancy, and that caused more friction.'

An understatement, Erin guessed.

'She said it was her body and none of my business,' he went on. 'She'd cut down on smoking, and, really, was it necessary to give up entirely? Weren't those health claims exaggerated? I had a professional opinion as well as a personal one, and both of those were ignored. She left...we split up...in April. He was born in August, a little underweight. I wasn't there. I first saw him when he was two days old.' There was a silence. 'And then came the custody dispute.'

'Right.'

'First she wanted him. Then she didn't want him. She wasn't getting any sleep. She wanted him half the time. She wasn't cut out for motherhood, and she'd told me that all along, so it was my fault. She wanted him on weekends. He was messing up her life. She wanted me to have him on weekends, and I'd pay half the cost of a nanny during the week. It went on and on, back and forth, hot and cold, but at least in the end we managed to avoid court. He was nearly a year old by the time the thing was finalised, with her giving up full custody to me, and so it wasn't until then that I could even begin to think about you.'

'No, I can see that.'

'Except, of course, I was,' he went on quietly. 'All the time.'

'Me, too.' Her voice was thin and low.

He stopped the car, swung onto an opportune stretch of gravel on the shoulder of the road and screeched to a halt, making the tyres pop as they scattered the gritty stones. He swore, his voice low and intense, a venting of all the frustration and uncertainty he'd felt over the past two years and more. And then he kissed her.

Nothing tentative or careful or sensible about it this time.

He reached across the gap between the bucket seats. The handbrake must have dug into his thigh, but he ignored it. He wrapped his arms around her, groaned and crushed his mouth against hers. Erin shuddered and began to cry. Hadn't known until now that you could kiss a man while sobbing your heart out and still feel as if every touch of skin on skin was setting you on fire.

'Don't cry, Erin,' he begged. He pressed his forehead against hers, rubbed his slightly roughened cheek along her jaw then claimed her lips again. 'Don't cry, darling love.'

'Let me,' she sobbed, then branded more hungry, mouth-trembling kisses onto his face, tasting him and not certain that she'd ever have enough of it, claiming every inch of him with her hands. 'I've spent two years not letting myself cry about you. Don't you dare try and spoil my pleasure now!'

He laughed. Their noses bumped, and then their mouths.

'I can't believe this,' she went on, her voice still jerky and her shoulders shuddering. 'My heart had started to scar over. I was trying so hard. I was supposed to go out with someone. Brother of someone at work. People are always trying to fix me up with their brothers, Alec!'

'Sometimes it works,' he put in softly.

'Does not! Mel was trying to fix me up with Simon, not you.'

'The principle's the same.'

She waved this aside, and went on, 'Next weekend, our date was supposed to be, but I've cancelled it. So I guess…'

She looked up at him, knew her eyes would be glowing out like the blue light on a police car in the middle of tear-reddened and swollen lids. Didn't even care, because all she saw in his face was love and happiness, an openness and triumph and exultation she'd seen in him so rarely, and never when he'd been looking at Kate.

'I *did* drop, didn't I?'

He understood at once. 'Yes, my gorgeous, passionate purple plum, you dropped, ripe and sweet and wonderful, into my desperate waiting hand, and if you hadn't, I don't know what I would have done. Really don't know. Don't want to think about it or talk about it or—'

Or even finished his sentence in any coherent way. He had more important things to do with his mouth after all. It was another ten minutes before they were ready to drive on, and when they did it was as if the wheels of the car didn't touch the ground.

CHAPTER THREE

THEY stopped first at a picnic area on Paddy's River, where the cool, clear stream tumbled around rocks and glided, sunny and shallow, over an old concrete causeway.

William was still asleep in the back of Alec's green Volvo, so he parked in the shade and they left all four doors open while they explored close by. There were late handfuls of ripe, unsprayed blackberries still hanging fat and shiny on a vast tangled maze of dusty berry bushes, so they picked some, staining their fingers purple, and washed them in the river.

'Juicy and sweet' was Alec's verdict. 'But a bit too seedy.'

'Don't want to collect some for jam or pies?'

'Better things to do today.' He grinned, and Erin could hardly take her eyes off his mouth as he popped another berry in then licked a tiny juice stain from his full, firm lower lip.

William awoke from his nap, disoriented and in tears for a few minutes. He had a red pressure mark on his cheek. Alec held him and bounced him and talked to him until he was smiling and talking, happy again. The sun shone on both their faces and brought out the golden glints in their hair.

Erin thought to herself, How could any woman give up this darling little boy? She felt a sudden spurt of dark, unpleasant feeling against Kate Gilchrist Rostrevor which frightened her.

'Can he paddle?' Alec asked. 'Is it safe?'

'Safe?'

'Yes. You know. Water snakes. Water spiders.'

'Water *spiders*?' She laughed.

'No, seriously, Australia does have a reputation for venomous—'

'It's safe, Alec.'

'Right. Great. As long as you're sure.' He grinned doubtfully. Crookedly, too, so that he might have been teasing.

'I promise I'm absolutely sure,' she told him seriously.

'OK, then. Think I'd prefer the possibility of tigers or rutting hippos somehow,' he muttered under his breath.

Erin laughed.

Expertly, he took off William's shoes, socks and trousers and held him by the hand as he toddled down to the causeway with his little nappy-clad bottom waggling from side to side.

William loved the water. He stomped up and down, shrieked with laughter, tried to catch the braided patterns of light and water as they streamed over the dark gold concrete. It had been stained like an old teacup by the trace of eucalyptus in the water.

Alec had taken off his shoes and socks, too, and had rolled his jeans to the knee, revealing well-muscled legs sprinkled with dark hair. He held William's hand, bending to smile or point, lift the little boy back safely from the causeway's edge or carry him out of the way once or twice when a car wanted to cross to one of the picnic tables on the opposite side.

The two of them paddled for about twenty minutes, during which Erin simply sat on a nearby rock in the sun and watched, enjoying the idyllic scene. She loved the lines Alec's body fell into when he bent and crouched beside his son, loved the serious attention he gave to William's every utterance.

'Water! Stick! 'Eaf!'

'Yes, that's right. Here comes a leaf, floating in the water.'

She'd planned originally to paddle herself. She had her feet bare and ready. But in the end she didn't, contenting herself with Alec's occasional brief smile in her direction. He seemed like a caring, involved dad, despite what he'd said the other day about how hard it was to be a single parent, and about his doubts.

Later, she was to look back on this scene and perceive nuances of meaning in it that hadn't been apparent at first glance. But today... Today, she was happy.

When William had had enough, they piled back in the car and drove through more pine and eucalyptus forest and more sheep country until they reached the nature reserve. There, Erin had to promise Alec that the large, evil-eyed emus weren't venomous *or* rutting. 'Whatever that is.' Although admittedly they were rather a nuisance as they brazenly attempted to make off with the barbecued sausages. He parried them with a pair of barbecue tongs and a lunge that proved he'd learned fencing at school.

'Very swashbuckling,' she told him. 'You'll make an excellent Australian, eventually.'

Snakes were a different story. Erin earnestly attempted to convince Alec that the dark creature—a red-bellied black—which slithered away into the grass at one point as they explored the wooded hill near the barbecue area after lunch was, in fact, *much* more scared of them than they were of it, but Alec was immune to this logic.

'How do you know?' he muttered darkly. 'I could be very scared indeed—for William's sake, of course.'

'Well, for William's sake, then,' she agreed kindly, 'we'll go for a hike on one of the forest creek trails where it will be too cool and shady for most of them.'

'Ah. *Most* of them.'

Alec put William up in a special backpack, then told Erin, 'The track looks pretty narrow. Do you want to go first?'

'To scare the snakes? Is that it?'

'Can I pretend it's really so I can look at that very nice wiggle in your walk?'

'Of course.'

'What an Amazon!'

She grinned. 'Thank you!'

And there it was again. A flash of Kate in Erin's mind. A moment of comparison. Had he ever called Kate 'an Amazon' with that hot, admiring light deep in his eyes? There came a sense of smug victory, followed by a nauseating wave of uncertainty.

Yes, we're so different, Kate and I. He thought he loved her once.

And why wouldn't he? Kate had turned down several very successful men in favour of him, Mel had said. They'd made a gorgeous couple. They'd married. They'd had a child. And this was so new.

A moment later, he stole a kiss, long and sweet and teasing. Then he walked beside her, tangling his fingers with hers and caressing the back of her hand with his thumb, as if he weren't wary of the snakes after all. She strongly suspected he'd been teasing her about his fear all along. He wasn't scared at all!

They didn't see any of the creatures, and they talked about marriage.

'Do you want to make it pretty soon?' he said.

He hadn't actually proposed, and she hadn't actually said yes. There had been something from him about it being a good idea, which she had agreed about at once. He'd given some energetically articulated reasons, even though she hadn't been arguing. Their position at the hospital. Mending fences with his parents in England. Stability for William. Something concrete and real, after all this waiting and doubt.

It had all made so much sense that they'd moved on at once from the question of *if* to the issue of when and how, with all the associated practicalities.

'How soon?' she asked.

'A month?' he suggested. 'Could we do it in a month?'

'I'm presuming you don't want—'

'A big wedding?' He shuddered, and a closed look that

she wasn't happy about passed briefly across his face. 'No. I'm not going through that again, thanks very much!'

And because there was so much else at stake, she surrendered some wedding fantasies that she hadn't even known she possessed, scaled down her dreams and didn't think about it any more. Of course he didn't want a big wedding after the first time.

'What were you thinking then?' she asked.

'Well, I'm only renting at this stage, but the place has a pretty nice back garden, so we could have it there. Drinks and nibbles, with a few people, then go on to a restaurant. Something like that.'

'How many people is a few?'

'Whoever you want.'

'I'd better book somewhere, then, because I do have a pretty large family.'

'And get yourself a dress.'

'Off the rack. There won't be time to order something specially made.'

'You don't know anyone who sews?'

'Not that well! Who'll come from your side, Alec?'

'Mel, if we're lucky. No one else. My parents aren't going to soften on this subject for a while.'

'Understatement?' she suggested.

'Understatement,' he agreed. 'Simon's serving overseas, but I'll get in touch with him just in case. Remember Christopher?'

'Your friend from school, in the bridal party.'

'I'll ask him, but he's pretty busy.'

'Mainly my side, then.'

'I don't mind. Not a bit.' It sounded a little too sincerely meant.

'And a honeymoon?' she pressed.

Silence.

'Alec?'

'Sorry. Bad memories associated with that word. Postpone it? I've only just started the job. I'm not due for leave.'

'Next summer, then, I suppose.' Her voice had got smaller.

He stopped in the middle of the walking track, beneath the half-curled frond of a tall and ancient tree-fern. Ahead, as yet unseen, a creek gurgled musically. The shade was cool and damp and pungent with the earthy odour of growth and decay. Some dappled light moved on Alec's face as he studied her, and the glimpses of sky overhead were brilliantly blue.

'Erin?' he said finally, lifting her chin with his cupped hand. He stroked her jaw, his fingers feather-light. Her spine tingled.

'Mmm?' was all she could manage.

'I'm not going to get my priorities wrong this time, OK?' he went on softly. 'Those are trappings. They don't matter.' He moved even closer, into full shade. He was still watching her closely, his eyes serious, his pupils large and dark in the dim, cool light. 'What matters is that we do this and get on with our lives together. Don't you agree?'

'Yes, I do agree,' she answered him steadily, fighting for it to make sense with her heart as well as her head. 'You're right.'

'Do you really want to put off the wedding until next summer so you can get your own personal silk meringue of a dress manufactured, and have bad, sugary poems printed on the table napkins, and wing off for two weeks in Hawaii? What would I do with William during that time, anyway?'

'We'd take him with us, of course.' She'd assumed that automatically. 'But I agree, Alec. There's no point in having all that fuss or waiting that long.'

And certainly not in having meringue dresses and bad poems.

'Couldn't wait if I tried, I don't think,' he muttered, and kissed her. It was just a brief, tantalising brush of his mouth, with William in the backpack an awkward interloper over his shoulder. 'I'm fighting to make up for lost time.'

How could any sane woman argue with that?

They had more things to arrange, and by the end of the hike it was all done, all the decisions were made and the tasks and priorities parcelled out.

After the wedding, Erin would give up her town house and move in with Alec. Since her lease still had another three months to run, she could do it at a leisurely pace, which took some of the pressure off. No scramble to organise movers, sell duplicate possessions and clean the place out over the next few hectic weeks.

She would organise the dress, the invitations and the flowers. Alec would take care of finding a suitable restaurant, ordering drinks and hors d'oeuvres, dealing with the paperwork and booking a civil marriage celebrant. He'd phone Mel, Simon and Christopher. His parents, too, and Kate, although he didn't expect either of those to be pleasant or productive calls.

When they arrived back at his car after their walk, Erin's head was buzzing and she felt exhausted, and it wasn't from the exertion of the walk.

Alec swung William and the backpack down off his shoulders, unstrapped the little boy and put him into his car seat once more.

'Koalas and kangaroos?' he said. 'Just quickly? The day's still glorious, but I don't want to tire him out.'

She almost said, What about tiring *me* out, after all we've talked about? But instead, after a moment, she simply nodded.

Poised to open the driver's side door, he stilled, then came around the front of the car to where Erin stood by the passenger door. He took her gently into his arms and they stood for quite some time without moving at all. With her ear pressed against his chest, she could hear the solid thud of his heart and could smell the sun-heated fabric of his shirt.

She didn't want to stir. Didn't even want to breathe. Just wanted to feel him, rediscover the rightness of this. His thighs anchored and supported her, and she could feel his arousal, matching her own aching, tangible need.

'Alec. Alec...' It was so good to have the right to speak his name like this, at last.

He kissed the top of her head and noted the same thing she had noticed in relation to his shirt. 'The sun's amazing,' he said. 'Your hair is actually hot from it. I can smell the heat and the fragrance.' He buried his face there. 'Never quite realised that sunshine had a smell before. I like this country of yours.'

She didn't answer. Didn't want to talk. They'd talked all the way through their walk and now she just wanted the peace. He seemed to understand.

'Sorry to bulldoze you through all that,' he said quietly, after a moment.

'You didn't. Not really,' she told him.

'But the situation did.'

'Was that it? Was it the situation?'

'Think so. Something like that.'

'OK...' She nodded.

'*Is* it, though?' he pressed. 'OK, I mean?'

'Yes. It is.' And she meant it, at heart. 'Just let me keep listening to your heartbeat.'

'As long as you want, darling.'

William wasn't happy, though. He squawked a couple of times, then started saying, 'Da-ddy! Da-ddy!' At the same time he tried to wriggle free of the car seat's restraining straps.

'Going to see animals now, Will. Kangaroos!' Alec enthused. And William was content again once the car was moving.

They spent an hour walking through the large open-range kangaroo and koala enclosures. Spotted two mother-and-baby koala pairs high in the forks of two eucalypts, and came close to a large pod of grey kangaroos sunning themselves on the dusty ground. Alec and William were both happy with the experience, and William slept again briefly on the journey home.

Erin stayed at Alec's house for the evening, and they ordered in some pizza and each drank a glass of wine. William had eggs and toast fingers and fruit, as well as a tentative triangle of pizza.

At a quarter to eight, Alec said apologetically, 'I'd better put him to bed. It takes a while. Do you want to wait?'

'I can clear up.'

'You don't have to.'

'Or… Could I read him a story?'

'I'll do it,' Alec said. 'We're in a routine with it all now.'

Erin nodded silently. They looked good together, father and son. They looked as if they belonged. William was locked onto Alec's hip, happy to survey the world from that position. He looked sleepy and very willing about the imminent journey to bed, knowing the 'routine' that Alec had spoken of.

'Night-night, William,' Erin said.

'Wave night-night, William,' Alec prompted.

'Ni'-ni'.' The little hand came up to flap up and down as it was supposed to, and off they went.

Erin cleared up, listening to the occasional sounds that floated back to her from the bedroom end of the house. Water ran. William squawked and sang. Alec spoke. 'Hold still, chum. It takes twice as long as it needs to when you wriggle like that.' A door closed. Voices murmured. A light switch clicked.

And Erin wasn't a necessary part of any of it. Even the

clearing up took her only a few minutes. But after all, she reminded herself, this was the first day.

Yes, and they'd be married in just over a month. Thirty-five days from now, in fact. And she'd be living here in this quiet, carpeted three-bedroom brown brick house, with its safe, sunny lawn at the back, its fenced yard, its double brick garage, its gauzy white curtains and its open fireplace.

She would be Alec's wife. Sharing his bed. Sharing William and that routine of his. It was wonderful. It was what she wanted. Her emotional life had turned around so fast that she was dizzy and breathless with astonishment and happiness.

But it didn't seem real.

'Have you met that hunky new Brit yet?' Siobhan Dixon asked.

She and Erin were sitting at the nurses' station on a quiet Monday evening, catching up on paperwork. There were two women in early first-time labour and another, under Leigh Ryan's care, who was almost ready to be taken with her baby to the postpartum ward.

'Alec Rostrevor?' Erin said. 'Uh…'

'Lovely name!' Siobhan sighed. 'He seems so nice, too. Confident, but not under the impression that he's lord of all things, the way a couple of them are. I'm sort of wondering if he's—'

'Yes, I have met him,' Erin got in desperately at last. 'I'm going to marry him, actually.'

Siobhan laughed. 'I love a girl with ambition!' She added another line of writing to a patient's chart.

'No…' Erin blushed. 'I mean, I *am* going to marry him. I knew him in England. We're engaged.'

Siobhan's mouth dropped open with an audible click and her pen fell from her fingers. 'Oh.'

'That's why he's here.'

'You mean he *followed* you, to—'

'Yes.'

'Wow!'

'It's not wow. I mean, it is, but—'

'Sorry, I didn't mean to tread on your toes just now, talking about him being—'

'You didn't, but—'

'Can I tell people?'

'You'd better.'

'Because you don't want anyone else mooning over him the way I just did, before they've had a chance to find out what's going on?'

'Yes. You see, we're getting married in just over four weeks.'

Silence, bristling with curiosity. Erin could practically see Siobhan calculating dates.

'I'm not pregnant,' she blurted. 'We just didn't want to wait.'

'Because of gossip.'

'Because of a whole lot of things. He's been married before, and he has a child. It's going to be a very small wedding.'

'Will his family come out for it? They're all in England, right?'

'Just his sister, it looks like.'

'Nice?' Siobhan picked up her pen again.

'Yes, Mel's terrific. We were friends before I knew Alec.'

'You see! People *do* fall in love with their friends' brothers. Ah…' Another pause for thought. 'Is that why you were reluctant about Callum?'

'Er, yes. You see at that stage— But don't worry,' Erin interrupted herself. 'I've already phoned Callum to cancel. Thanks for—'

'He broke your heart, didn't he?' Siobhan breathed. Once more, the pen skittered onto the desk. 'Wow! And then he realised what he'd lost, that he loved you after all, and he came out here to lay siege to your heart and win you, and he did. That's—'

'It's not wow, OK? It's really not. It all…just happened. Not really quite the way you said. He has his young son who needs stability. We've tried to make sensible plans.'

'Oh, of course. Absolutely. I think it's fabulous news, Erin, I really do.'

And Siobhan did. Erin knew it and was grateful for it. She just wished there hadn't been quite so many people, over the past two days, who had greeted the news of her impending wedding with such open-mouthed astonishment, despite the delight that went with it. Even her sister Caitlin, who had connived with Mel Rostrevor to bring the whole thing into being, had confessed that she hadn't expected the matter to be concluded so soon.

'Why not?' Erin had retorted during their phone conversation last night. 'You and Angus were pretty quick on the draw once you found out about Scott's infidelity, Caitlin.'

'True. True, but— Well, never mind. I just thought you might have had some more issues to work through first, that's all. I told Alec to take it slowly, and to be very cautious.'

'Well… It just didn't happen like that.'

And now here was kind-hearted Siobhan, instantly forgiving Erin over the matter of her brother and acting as if this was something out of a movie in which Erin was the star. The same reaction spread like an illness amongst the rest of the hospital staff over the next couple of days.

Erin realised that she had to tell people in a formal sort of way, rather than simply letting the news slip out as she'd let it slip to Siobhan. Alec agreed, and began to tell people as well. That they'd known each other in England but the timing hadn't been right, and that he'd followed her here two years later to try and win her heart.

The number of souls around the hospital who seemed genuinely interested took them both by surprise. Laid-back orderlies, senior obstetricians, motherly diet maids with European accents—all of these people turned out to have hidden veins of romance inside them, like seams of gold in a block of quartz, and they were brought to the surface by this story of lovers divided in one hemisphere and reunited in another.

Nobody mentioned the as yet unworded fears which lurked on the edges of Erin's awareness, and since she didn't fully understand them herself she sort of stepped around them in her mind. Sidled past. Closed her eyes. Filed them in the 'too-hard' basket.

In a medical environment, this wasn't, of course, a piece of procrastination you could engage in when it came to your work. Crises happened when they happened, and you had to deal with them on the spot.

On Wednesday a young, single mother-to-be was admitted via the accident and emergency department, moved upstairs to the labour ward and assigned to Erin. Twenty-two-year-old Natalie Cross's prenatal care had been erratic and she was obviously an intravenous drug user. She was vague about her exact dates, but insisted that she was 'seven months gone. Due in May'.

Erin wasn't convinced. The top of the uterus should have been much higher if those dates were right. Beyond about twelve weeks, you could reach a pretty accurate estimate of gestational age by measuring the size of the pregnancy from pelvic bone to top of uterus and equating each centimetre with one week. Thirty centimetres equalled thirty weeks' gestation.

Erin stretched her tape measure across the pale, distended abdomen of her reluctant patient and found that Natalie measured twenty-one.

She called the resident, knowing it would be Alec and that he'd want to be here, and when he came she experienced for the hundredth time that wash of heat and lurch in her stomach that threw her off balance even while it confirmed everything she felt. Her world was *right* when he was in it. She couldn't explain how or why, it just *was*.

They smiled at each other, glowing with their secret. Didn't care if their patient saw the innocent moment.

She didn't. A contraction was coming and she was already in the grip of painful drug withdrawal, not in a mood to take more pain. She swore and cursed and writhed.

As soon as the contraction had eased, she said, 'Can I make a phone call? I need a friend to come in.'

Alec and Erin both knew what was in her mind. A hit.

'Would you like some pain relief first?' Alec asked gently. He knew as well as Erin did that this wasn't going to be a happy outcome.

'Yes! Anything!' Natalie said.

Erin prepared gas, which she knew wouldn't help much. Alec did an internal, saying, 'Let's see if you've got time for an epidural.' It was the only thing that really brought relief to drug-dependent mothers, as their bodies were too hardened to the effect of most other appropriate medications.

But Natalie didn't have time for an epidural. The baby was coming, and the mother was out of control, unable to focus on managing her pain or her pushing in any way. Fortunately, her body did most of the work on its own. With each contraction, the uterus humped up into a tight, rock-hard ball and Natalie strained downwards instinctively, bringing the tiny head low into the birth canal.

She kept up a ceaseless barrage of noise throughout. 'I need my friend to come in. Now!' she yelled between each contraction, while during them she simply screamed and bellowed, her face red and the tendons on her thin neck standing out.

It was obvious from the beginning that the baby wasn't going to make it. She was a tiny, unformed little girl, only at about twenty-three weeks' gestation, and small even for that. A big, healthy baby whose mother had been well nourished and had received good prenatal care could occasionally survive at that age without long-term health problems, but a small, badly nourished and heroin-addicted baby was a very different story.

She emerged limp and unresponsive, and though Erin had already paged a paediatrician some minutes earlier—Neil Watson arrived a minute or two after it was all over—nothing could be done. Alec diligently attempted resuscitation, but they both knew from the start that it wasn't going to work. Nobody wanted a baby to survive in these circumstances. Not even the mother.

Told that her baby was too small and hadn't lived, Natalie's first words were a driven, desperate, 'I need my friend to come in.'

Erin called the social worker and got out the unit's Polaroid camera to take some pictures of the baby, swaddled and nestled in her mother's arms. It could help people a little to have this memory.

Natalie seemed too strung out to care. She hardly seemed to hear what the social worker said to her, or notice Erin's help in getting her showered and comfortable. And when she finally phoned three different numbers, the 'friend' was unavailable and Natalie discharged herself against medical advice within two hours.

She had shown no emotion about her dead child, and had apparently left the maternity floor quite deliberately when no one had been looking. There were several channels which would have given her appropriate ongoing help and support. She had known of them, thanks to the social worker's input, but evidently she didn't want them. At least she had taken the Polaroid photos with her.

Meanwhile, Alec and Erin went through the formalities, and paediatrician Neil Watson returned to the neonatal unit.

After it was all taken care of, Erin was assigned to a happy first-time mother in relatively comfortable labour for the rest of her shift, which helped.

Going straight home to Alec's house afterwards helped more. He probably wouldn't be getting there until nearly six, but they had agreed that she would cook dinner and spend a couple of hours with William and his nanny, Alison. Alison would leave when Alec got home. There would be a short evening centred around William's needs.

And then Erin would spend the night. They'd talked about it yesterday, over lunch in the hospital cafeteria.

'Want to bring your toothbrush to my place tomorrow?' Alec had slid his hand across the table to hold and stroke Erin's as he'd said it.

'My toothbrush...'

'The toothbrush thing is a pretty important step,' he'd pointed out softly, 'when people are getting married.'

'It is, I know.'

'If you're not ready for it yet, we can wait. Till after the wedding, if you like.'

'Don't want to wait.'

'Sure? I didn't mean to push.'

'You didn't,' she'd assured him, running her fingertips across the back of his hand then letting them rest in his up-turned palm. 'Would have stayed the other night, if you'd asked.'

'I wanted to ask. Bit my tongue about six times. But hadn't I already pushed enough for one day?'

'No, Alec! I...have a very strong feeling I'm going to love the toothbrush thing with you.'

'Me, too,' he'd teased, his eyes warm and bright. 'Been imagining it, actually. Our two toothbrushes, side by side in the dark in the toothbrush rack.'

She'd laughed. 'Let's not carry this analogy any further,

because once you start talking about toothpaste and bristles, it really doesn't work for me.'

'You're right. Bit kinky.' He'd grinned, leaning towards her, his chin cupped in his hand. 'But you know what I meant.'

'Oh, I know what you meant.'

So she had brought her toothbrush and a change of clothing as well as several other things, and she had them in her overnight bag in the boot of her car. She had a cookbook sitting on the front passenger seat as well, with a list of ingredients stuck inside it like a bookmark, ready for a stop at the shops.

She was going to cook Italian. A bean and pasta soup which was so delicious he'd never suspect how easy it was, and a big bowl of fusilli tossed with prosciutto, broccolini and cherry tomatoes. If they were going to spend the rest of the evening celebrating the packing of Erin's toothbrush, they might as well do it on satisfied stomachs.

It was odd to be at Alec's house without Alec. Odd to change out of her uniform in his bedroom. It notched the intimacy and the reality of their relationship a little higher. Alison was making an afternoon snack for William when Erin emerged, wearing cropped black pants and a soft pink top. He had just woken from his nap, and there were bright toys scattered on the living room carpet in front of the brick fireplace from his earlier play.

Erin liked fifty-two-year-old Alison at once, and wondered why Alec had expressed that faint reserve when he'd first mentioned her. Distrusting of his own judgement? He was a parent, and parents were protective, over-cautious. He'd said it himself. Erin wasn't in that position.

Yet.

She could stand back enough to see the tenderness in Alison's handling of the little boy, the warmth in her smile

LILIAN DARCY 63

and the patience in the way she played with him. Alec didn't need to knot himself up with reservations.

'Could I take him for a walk?' she asked the older woman. 'Is there a playground near here?'

'There are some swings just up the road, in a little park. He'd love that, and I can get the house straightened out a little more. Dr Rostrevor is paying me as a nanny and house-keeper, but the housekeeping part tends to suffer at this little man's hands.'

'I'm sure Alec thinks that's the right priority on your part.'

William was busy getting all the saucepans out of the cup-boards one by one. He took them through to the large, low, hardwood coffee table in the sunny living room, and placed each lid on the correct pot with great satisfaction.

'He's going to help you cook,' Alison predicted.

'Lovely!'

'It'll take you twice as long.'

They both laughed, and Erin put William's hat on, popped him in his stroller and wheeled him off in the direction Alison had indicated. He went willingly, and they had a wonderful hour. Erin pushed William in the swing, then let him roam around the little park. He picked up sticks, studied insects and played 'Boo!' behind several big shaggy-barked gum trees.

Erin could have plotted the growth of her feelings on a graph. She'd gone beyond the cautious curiosity she had felt at first.

Alec's son. My soon-to-be stepson. My future husband's little boy.

Already now there were bonds forming, moments when her heart filled with a tender new sensation that was very welcome to her. There were memories of William that he and she were creating together, and that Alec didn't share. She'd have stories to tell Alec when he got home.

One story too many, as it turned out. They were almost

ready to leave when William ran across the cement pathway that traversed the park, tripped on an uneven crack and fell, grazing his palms and knees and giving himself a fat, bleeding lip which he wouldn't let Erin examine.

He cried all the way home, his face streaming and the front of his little striped T-shirt getting wet and stained. Erin had folded the umbrella-style stroller and hooked it over her arm. She carried him every step, becoming aware as they went that he needed a serious nappy change as well.

As they walked, she kissed his little head to soothe him. Oh, that hair was so fine and silky and gorgeous! She murmured lots of reassuring words as well, but they didn't seem to help. He was at a clingy age, she was almost a stranger to him, and he didn't want her.

Her arms were aching by the time they got home and her heart was aching, too, with remorse. Alison must have heard the crying—the whole street had, no doubt—because she was standing in the open doorway with an anxious look on her face as Erin stumbled up the steps.

'What happened?' Alison took him at once and he went with his arms stretched out to her, his sobs even louder than before.

'He fell on the cement path. I'm so sorry.'

Which made it sound as if she'd broken someone else's plate, or something. A mother wouldn't have apologised like that.

'It happens, love,' Alison said. 'They're not steady on their feet at that age, and they will run. Can't help themselves. It won't be the first time.'

'Will Alec be—?' Erin began, but Alison hadn't heard. She had turned with William still in her arms to take him along to the bathroom.

Angry, Erin had been going to say. Will Alec be angry?

That's stupid, to think of it that way, she decided. But *will* he? I'm still worried about it. Again, it's as if I'd broken a precious plate. How long is it going to take us to get the hang of this?

In the bathroom, Alison had William standing on the vanity unit in front of the mirror and was sponging the dirt out of the cuts and grazes and rinsing the blood from his mouth.

'His front teeth feel loose,' she said.

'Oh, no!'

'You're a nurse. Do you know what it means? Should we take him to the dentist or the hospital? Look, his gums around those teeth are all swollen and purple.'

'I—I have no idea about it,' Erin stammered. 'I haven't done much paediatric nursing. I think they'll probably set back in, but I— Does Alec have a dentist? Can we phone and ask?'

They heard Alec's key in the lock at that moment. Home early. It was only just after five. William was still crying, and Alec came straight towards the sound, appearing in the bathroom doorway after only a few seconds, to ask bluntly, 'What happened?'

Erin explained.

And when he wasn't even remotely angry but simply concerned—for William first and foremost, of course, but for Erin as well—she was so relieved that she felt even shakier than before.

'Let me have a look at him, Alison,' Alec said calmly. 'You can go now, if you want. We'll handle things.'

'Yes, all right.' She went to get her bag.

'William, little man, let Daddy have a look in your mouth.' His eyes were focused steadfastly on his son, then he turned his head. 'Erin, did you have to carry him all the way home?'

'That was the ea-easy part!' Her voice cracked. 'I felt so…' She didn't finish, still hugely upset over the whole thing. Her legs were shaky and there was a lump in her throat. She could have howled along with William. Reining it in, she said, 'He needs a fresh nappy, too, Alec, but we haven't got to that yet.'

He had stopped crying at least, though his breathing was still jerky and his little shoulders shuddering. He let Alec gently lift his swollen top lip and touch the teeth. 'Bit of a jiggle, isn't there?' he said. 'I've seen it before, though, in Casualty in London. Nothing to do at this stage. If they change colour, the nerves may be affected, but otherwise they should firm up over the next week or so. The fibres that hold them in place will knit in children.'

'He's grazed as well.'

'Tomorrow as usual, Dr Rostrevor?' Alison asked, appearing back in the doorway.

Alec nodded. 'Thanks, Alison. See you then.'

Erin said goodbye and William gave a half-hearted wave until his hand was captured and examined by his father. 'Very shallow, and you've got them nice and clean. Want some Band-Aids, little love?'

'Bam-bay.'

'Yes, lots of lovely bam-bays, on all your grazes. That'll tell you it's not the first time, Erin, the fact that he knows the word.'

He gave her a quick kiss, landing half on her mouth and half on her cheek, followed by a rueful smile. Then he saw the complex mix of doubt and relief in her eyes and kissed her again more sweetly.

'Want to do something to help?' he murmured, his eyes hotly examining her mouth as if he might not be able to resist kissing it for a third time.

'Yes, please!'

'Start cooking, because I skipped lunch and I'm going to be starving for dinner. I'll fix his nappy and be out in a minute.'

Ten minutes, actually, by which time Erin had calmed down, started the soup and—almost—forgiven herself.

CHAPTER FOUR

SOFT music on the CD player, soft lighting over the dining table, wine red and rich in stemmed crystal glasses...

William had tired himself out with crying so he'd eaten some soup at six and gone to bed an hour early. They had eaten Erin's meal. Alec was gratifyingly impressed, and they had lingered at the table talking for more than an hour, exchanging facts and memories from their lives that they hadn't had a chance to mention until now. So much of what had happened between them until this point was based on intuition.

It was as if they had known they loved each other before they'd worked out why. Their hearts and their senses had gone racing on ahead, blazing with confidence and certainty. Now their lives had to catch up.

A silence had fallen. Erin didn't want any more wine. She wanted Alec. He must have felt the same.

'Where's that toothbrush of yours?' he asked her softly.

'In my overnight bag.'

'Put it in the bathroom next to mine?'

'Poor toothbrush! Is it lonely?'

'That's where it belongs, Erin.'

He lifted her hand to his lips across the table. She stood up. So did he, and in a few not quite steady steps they'd come together, clinging to each other and capturing deep, hungry kisses. Their hips bumped, their breathing was shallow and erratic and Erin's heart thudded slow and hard.

'How do we do this, Erin?' Alec asked in an uneven voice, brushing his mouth against her ear. 'I want to set the right foundation, make it magic.'

67

'Oh, it will be.'

'Should I just pick you up and take you to the bedroom?'

He was scooping her up before she had a chance to answer, one forearm beneath her thighs and his other hand nudging her breast. She laughed as she buried her face in the warmth of his neck.

'This is a good start.'

Alec put her down again once they reached the well-ordered, masculine room, and they stood in the middle of it, silent and a little tentative now. The house was quiet and still. There was nothing to distract them from each other.

He bent to kiss her, printing his lips softly across her face, touching the corner of her mouth then taking it fully, teasing her with his tongue, letting his hands drift lightly down from her shoulders to reach her breasts. Deliberately he rubbed his thumbs across her nipples and they hardened at once.

He bent his head lower, opened his mouth and took the aching peaks through the fabric, one then the other, breathing out each time to create heat. Then he groaned and pulled impatiently at her top, lifting it to bunch softly beneath her arms. He cupped her breasts through her cotton and lace bra, but that still wasn't good enough. For either of them.

'Let me—' she began.

'No, please. Let *me*...'

He slid his hands around to her back and slipped the clasp open, cupping and caressing her as she clumsily pulled top and dangling bra over her head.

'How have I waited so long for this?' he rasped, raking his hands hungrily over her breasts so that she shuddered and arched back.

'I don't know,' she gasped. 'Don't know how I'm still alive...'

'You don't know what living is yet, Erin Gray!'

The husky threat sent coils of searing need looping through her and she reached out to pull on his shirt. She had never seen him naked. Never been close. Bathing suit one day that first summer—navy blue shorts clinging damply to his hips and thighs at a wealthy neighbour's indoor pool. The sight had haunted her for months. The reality of his skin here beneath her hands was magical and almost painful.

'Cold?'

'No.'

But she knew why he'd asked. His hands had grazed her breasts once more, to find them tight, swollen and straining even harder for his touch.

'We won't bother with the covers, then.'

But it was a long time before they got as far as the covers. Alec felt himself exquisitely poised between clamouring impatience and a sensual determination to take this slowly and savour every second of it. He knew that Erin wanted him. Hell, how could he have been in any doubt? She was shining with it, glowing and glistening with it. The valley between her softly rounded breasts was sheened with sweat, and her eyes were so wide and dark he could have drowned in them.

She had a purity to her, a radiant openness. He'd noticed it from the very beginning. Couldn't understand how it had taken him so long to recognise what it was in her that called him and what his response truly meant.

Kate had *never* made love like this.

He shuddered. Erin's hands were at his belt, her fingers slim, shaking yet deft. She was almost sobbing.

'Damn! Oh, Alec!' she muttered, then got it loose and slid his trousers down the sides of his thighs. 'I want you. I want this.'

'I know.' He heard the rasp in his voice, took a shuddering breath and pulled her against him.

Was almost undone by it, and sensed her mounting urgency, too. They clung together, not daring to move, then dragged themselves to the bed. She wasn't cold. They didn't need the covers. She was radiant with warmth. So was he.

The moment when they finally came together was painfully perfect. She lay back on the bed, her face hidden by her hair and by one arm flung across her eyes as if what she felt was too naked for even Alec himself to see.

Engulfed by her, he told himself he needed to hold back, but then found that he didn't. Erin was with him all the way, riding the same crest of tumbling, dizzying, dark, hot energy, pleading with him in phrases that made no sense. Oh, but he understood!

'Yes,' he said, on fire with the thought of it. 'Yes, my love.'

Then he couldn't say anything more.

Afterwards, Erin held him, his head pillowed against her breasts. He lay on his side with one leg flung across her, and she didn't care that the bone at the side of his knee pressed too hard on her thigh. He seemed to fill her arms completely, the way he'd filled a more intimate part of her just minutes earlier.

She opened her mouth and gave his shoulder a playful bite, like a kitten or a toothless child, and he moved a little to kiss her jaw.

We belong to each other, she thought. He belongs to me. This magic between us is only ours.

There were other times in her life when she had done this—had lain in bed with a man after love-making. Not many times. And nothing that had ever possessed an ounce of this *rightness*.

My Alec. My body and his. As close as two bodies can ever be...

A few moments later, with no words necessary, and none spoken, he slept and so did she, utterly content.

Later, waking gradually after the surrender of sleep, it seemed natural to shelter, cosily entwined, beneath smooth sheets and puffy quilt, and their love-making this time was quieter, more tender, safer and even more magical.

This time, they didn't wake again until dawn, when William cried and Alec brought him into the bed.

'He'll snooze a bit more now. Do you mind? We can break the habit if you do. Some child-care books say you should never let them into your bed—hate child-care books, I've decided!' He grinned. 'But I love it when he opens his eyes at about seven and the very first thing that happens is a big smile and the word "Daddy". Or, lately, for some reason, "nose".'

'It's lovely, Alec,' she said. 'He's so warm and sweet.'

And too little to question the presence of a woman in his father's bed, clad only in a long, lacy nightgown. Since Alec had donned some very jaunty red flannel pyjamas at some point during the night, the whole thing was perfectly respectable, though their love-making had seemed anything but.

Erin shivered with desire at the thought of it, and wished for a few moments that she could have turned into Alec's arms once more. The whole bed was velvety and warm from their shared body heat. Then she surrendered her body's need and embraced the feeling…the belief, the hope, the possibility…that the three of them were a family, instead.

'Where's my nose, William?' she said.

The feeling that they were a family deepened significantly over the next few days. Several sets of clothing and other possessions joined Erin's pioneering toothbrush at Alec's place. Alison was commendably unruffled about this development, and there was no friction on that score.

Erin only stayed one of the four nights at home. In theory, this was to get some sleep, since she and Alec hadn't been doing very much of that at his place. They'd made love, eaten decadent chocolate treats in bed, talked and made love again, far into the night. Back in her own bed on Saturday night, however, she was restless and awash with relived sensation.

It would probably have been easier to sleep with Alec himself beside her.

On Sunday, Erin's brother Gordon and his wife Rachel had the three of them over to a barbecue at their place. Their parents came up from their beachside home on the South Coast for the event and welcomed Alec and William into their lives with a comfortable warmth and lack of fuss.

William and Archie got on beautifully, as they were only about six months apart in age. Another of Erin's brothers, Peter, was there as well, with his wife Lisa and slightly older children.

The sun was shining, the food was lovely, and lots of family news was exchanged.

'I think Caitlin might be pregnant again,' Mum reported. 'She and Angus were down last weekend.'

'Neither of them have said anything to me about it,' Rachel answered.

Angus was her brother, and there had been another instance of misguided sisterly matchmaking two years earlier, when she had tried to fix him up with Erin. Wrong sister. Freshly arrived back from London, Erin's heart had already been lost to Alec. From the beginning, Angus hadn't been interested, and had married Caitlin instead.

'No, well, she didn't to me, either,' Mum agreed. 'But she seemed a little fragile, and Angus was treating her as if she were made of glass.'

'Don't we all, when she'll let us,' Rachel sighed. 'Oh, I hope you're right. And I can understand their not saying anything.' She lowered her voice. 'Erin, you're getting one ready-made.'

They both looked across the bright Australian native garden to where Alec was playing with William on Archie's swing-set. His grazes had healed, the swelling in his lip had gone down and his teeth had stayed the right colour. No one

would have guessed that it was only four days since he had
hurt himself.

'Is that going to be all right?' Rachel went on.

'For Caitlin?' Erin queried. 'You know she's not as petty
as that.'

'That's not what I meant. I'm talking about you. A child
changes the balance in the relationship, even when it's your
own. William will be your stepson. And I have to say I'm
pretty curious about the ex-wife. The lovely, sophisticated
Kate. Doesn't she want anything to do with him at all?'

'Apparently not. She's very focused on her career. Has
another film coming up, or something.'

'Or something? You don't know the details?'

'We don't talk much about Kate.'

'Ah.'

'We have better things to discuss, Rachel!'

'I know you do. But that Kate creature makes me nervous.'

'She's not a creature, she's William's mother. She's involved in this, and I'm trying very hard not to develop a—'

'Rachel's sticking up for you, Erin,' Gordon put in mildly,
edging his chair closer.

'Yes. OK. I know you are,' Erin told her sister-in-law,
laying a hand on her bare, tanned forearm. 'And I appreciate
it. I'm a little defensive, I suppose.'

'Pre-wedding nerves?'

'Something like that.'

It was the only note of awkwardness during the afternoon,
and they stayed quite late, lazing on the large timber deck,
surrounded by wattles, bottlebrush and gum trees. William
hadn't napped. He was ragged with exhaustion and Erin and
Alec both expected him to conk out in his car seat on the
way home, but he didn't. He sang to himself, chatted nonsense at the cars and looked very pink-cheeked.

'Although I put sunscreen on him,' Alec said. 'And a hat.'

'Is he feverish?' Erin suggested, and when they felt his little forehead at home, her theory was confirmed.

'Not enough to worry about,' Alec concluded. 'I'll give him something mild to bring it down.'

William fell asleep at last an hour later, at five o'clock, slept through until seven the next morning without a peep, and woke up with chickenpox.

Three spots at this point, classic pink watery blisters in the warm, moist area around his groin. Erin found them when she changed his nappy—a task which she'd become quite good at in the space of three or four attempts since Wednesday.

'Not your week, is it, little chum?' she told him, and called Alec, who was just coming out of the shower.

'He's not feverish any more,' he observed.

'No, he seems quite happy, actually.'

'They often are, unless it's a bad case. Which I hope this won't be. He must have picked it up at play-group.'

'He'll still be faintly spotty at the wedding, even if we give him oatmeal baths to ease the itching.'

'Not to worry.'

'I'm off today. Will I cancel Alison?' she offered. 'Take care of him myself?'

He stilled and looked at her. 'Would you like to? I haven't wanted to… I haven't known if you…'

Not the best setting for one of the most serious, important talks they'd ever had, standing together in the laundry in front of the big white washing machine, on which rested a towelling-covered change-pad with William wriggling impatiently on top of it.

Are you going to get me dressed, or what? he seemed to be saying. What's the fuss? *I* haven't noticed any spots.

'If I wanted to get that deeply involved?' Erin suggested, as an ending to Alec's second unfinished sentence in a row.

'Is that what you meant? Please, say it, tell me when there's something like this on your mind.'

'Yeah?' He seemed doubtful, as if it was more manly somehow to keep his worries to himself.

'I can't work in the dark. And I *am* involved, Alec. I'm already the closest thing this little guy has to a hands-on mother substitute. Started with the toothbrush thing, and—and—'

'Yes, that,' he said softly. 'That was bigger than I'd considered, making love to you so wonderfully, and then waking up to both William and you in the morning.'

'And it gets to a whole new level twenty-six days from now after the wedding,' she went on. 'You keep trying to make me do this gradually, but I can't, OK? I need to jump in at the deep end with this, the way I did when I fell in love with you.'

His attention caught on this admission for a moment, like a sock catching on a blackberry thorn. 'Did you? At the deep end?'

'Oh, you know that! Took about two days.'

'Me, too, when I think back. Only I didn't let myself see it.'

They grinned at each other in a silly sort of way, and their fingers tangled together, brushing against Erin's thigh. His nearness overwhelmed her, as always. His brief, hot kiss made her tremble.

'And you feel like that about William?' he pressed, still searching her face.

'I'm going to. I *want* to. I'm starting to, and I will. And the quickest way to do that is by being with him, taking care of him, doing all the things that mothers do. So let me, Alec, don't hold me back. What's the point of that? He doesn't have Kate any more. He needs me. And I *want* him to. I want to be William's mother.'

She had tears in her eyes by the time she finished.

'Oh, God, *do* you?' he breathed raggedly.

She nodded, closed her eyes and couldn't speak. She was aware of William threatening to crawl off the change-pad and plummet to the floor, felt Alec lift him quickly down and say absently, 'Go and play with your pots, William.'

'He hasn't got a nappy on,' she managed weakly, her eyes still closed.

'Don't care. At the moment this is more important. We need to talk. *Erin*!'

Apparently it was a talk they could have without words. He simply held her for what felt like quite a long time, so that she was swamped in his fresh-from-the-shower scent, a combination of soap, shampoo and plain, clean skin, overlaid with the indescribable tang of sun-dried cotton shirt.

At the edge of her awareness, she heard William playing nearby with his pots and pans in his usual absorbed fashion. It was a delightful sound, like the chirrup of birds or the gurgle of a stream, so happy and pretty.

Alec pressed his chin into the top of her head and slid his hands down her back, then brought his palms to rest against the backs of her upper thighs. His freshly shaven cheek nudged her ear, then his forehead dropped onto her shoulder and she ran her fingers through his damp, clean hair, scarcely able to breathe. Something had happened to her heart. It filled her whole chest, and it was circling love and need, not blood, through her body.

Sometimes she still couldn't believe that she now had the right to touch Alec like this, and that her touch could make him react so powerfully, every muscle hard and shaking.

Finally, he spoke.

'Kate…always treated William as such a liability,' he said with difficulty. 'Even at the times when she said she wanted him. It was as if she resented the fact that he'd made her love him. I didn't know…what you'd be able to feel for him. When he wasn't yours. When he was just thrust on you. Part of the package. I was protecting you from him being a nuisance, or something. And you're right. I didn't want to push. Don't like pushing. Got pushed myself, too much, in years past. I'm sorry.'

'It's all right.' It was all she said, but it was enough.

Something had changed and clarified for both of them, and it was good.

Meanwhile, over the next three days, William's skin blossomed with new spots every time they looked at him. Face, chest, groin, back, neck, thighs and ears. They even crept down between his toes and onto his tongue. He seemed barely to have noticed, and played happily as usual.

Since he loved his bath, he greeted the unexpected frequency of his trips to the tub with delight, and Erin cut one leg off an old pair of her pantihose, filled it with a handful of oats for each bath and squeezed the smooth, milky starch into the water and onto his skin. Alison and Alec did the same when William was in their care.

This eased the itching, which reduced the likelihood of infection from little scratching fingers, and Erin knew that most of the blisters would not scar. By Thursday, the spots had crusted over and no new ones were appearing, which meant he was no longer infectious.

'Nice to have it over with,' Alec said to Erin somewhat complacently. He had his arm wrapped around her in bed, and he was cupping her breast, making silky movements with his fingers on her sensitive skin. 'It was a bad enough case that he won't get it again, as some children do when they've had a mild dose.'

'Mmm, that's good,' she said, and it came out so cat-like, ambiguous and seductive that they forgot about William for the moment and focused on…other things.

Plans for the wedding and their future together came to the fore once more over the following days. As Alec had expected, neither Christopher nor Simon were available. Mel was coming, arriving the day before the ceremony and planning a stay of two weeks. She would travel within Australia for part of that time, she said.

Mr and Mrs Rostrevor wouldn't be there. Alec had shut himself in his study one evening to phone them, only to emerge twenty minutes later with a tight, pale face, a clamped mouth and no report beyond, 'They're not coming.'

Erin managed not to press for more detail and tried not to take her future in-laws' decision too personally. The Rostrevors had always been charming to her during her visits with Mel, but she strongly suspected they felt differently about her now. They were a strong-minded couple, and charm could be a two-edged sword.

'Great that Mel can make it, though,' Alec said.

He'd booked a table for twenty at a nearby French restaurant, and a night for just the two of them in an expensive hotel near Parliament House. Mel would look after William overnight.

All of Erin's immediate family were coming, as well as several friends, and with Rachel's help she had found a cream shantung silk dress that she loved. It had a simply cut sleeveless bodice with a wide, curved neckline and a fitted waist opening into a full, calf-length skirt with an underlayer of tulle.

Mum had already made a traditional fruit cake and delivered it to a professional decorator. Since Alec was busy at work, Erin had taken over some of the tasks he had planned to handle, and had enjoyed them all more than she wanted to admit. But, then, she was floating through everything at the moment in a state of dreamy, disbelieving happiness.

The florist had shown her page upon page of photos of bouquets, then suggested roses, ageratum and creamy, many-petalled flannel flowers. A caterer was handling drinks and hors d'oeuvres in the garden, which would receive several hours of extra attention from Alec's gardening service the day before the event. Mel was to be bridesmaid and Caitlin matron of honour. Gordon would be best man and Peter Mel's groomsman partner.

Erin no longer regretted the loss of church, veil, professional photographer, printed invitations and Hawaiian honeymoon. She went to work on light feet, felt happily tearful at every baby she helped bring into the world and melted every time Alec crossed her path in the unit.

Half her things were at his place now. He'd bought a chest of drawers for her, as her bedroom furniture from the town house was built in. On the rare nights when she stayed at her place, usually only after a late or back-to-back shift, she would invariably discover that the shoes she wanted to wear the next day were no longer there.

She had just made this same discovery in relation to a certain cotton cardigan on the Wednesday morning before the wedding when Alec phoned. A little early, actually, since he knew she'd worked until eleven the previous night. It was not yet eight, and she might easily have still been in bed.

'Did William seem all right to you yesterday?' he wanted to know at once.

She had taken care of the little boy until it had been time to leave for work in the middle of the afternoon, when Alison had taken over until Alec's return.

'Yes, fine, why?'

'Oh, he doesn't seem quite himself this morning, that's all. I can't put my finger on it.'

'Feverish?'

'No, temperature's quite normal. Can't feel any teeth coming. But he's out of sorts. He's had a couple of falls already. Something's bothering him.'

'I'll come over.'

'Wondered if you wanted to have breakfast, anyway. I'm off today.'

'That's right.'

He had worked all weekend, and she'd spent most of it with William. He still had the pinkish-purple remnants of chickenpox spots all over him, but they were fading more each day.

'Sorry to ring so early, but I just—' He broke off. In the background, Erin heard a clatter and crying. 'There he goes again. I can't work out why it's happening. He's not tripping over anything. Now he's just sitting in the middle of the floor in tears.'

'I'll be there soon.'

'Not too soon, because I'm going out to get croissants.'

'You actually don't *want* my dress to fit on Saturday, do you?' she teased, and when she got there half an hour later, he had relaxed a little on the issue of William.

'He seems fine now. I'm too much of a doctor, that's the trouble.' Alec kissed her absently, frowning, and didn't stay long enough for her to hold him in her arms. 'Look at him, sitting on the couch, listening to his music and looking at his book! Little angel. Perhaps it's the new shoes. Alison bought them yesterday, and this is the first time he's had them on. I wish they could tell you what's wrong. Wonder sometimes if at some level he still misses Kate…'

'I expect that would be natural,' Erin agreed, with a rather jerky nod.

But it wasn't that, and there *was* something wrong.

They weren't certain of it that day. William was fairly quiet during the morning, occasionally fretful—mainly, it seemed, when he was active. They took the new shoes off, and he sat on the floor and played happily with blocks.

'OK, it's just the shoes,' Alec decided. 'Too stiff.'

He checked William's feet for blisters, but there weren't any. William ate lunch and had his nap, during which Erin went off to work.

'Coming here tonight?' Alec wanted to know.

'I'll be late,' she said.

'Don't care.'

So she folded herself into bed beside him at eleven forty-five that night and he cuddled up against her, all warm and sleepy and naked, at once. 'How's William?' she asked.

'Asleep. Seems fine. I'm going to take him to the doctor tomorrow.'

'Because he seems fine? And, Alec, you *are* the doctor.'

'No. In this case, I'm the parent. I'm going to see if David Kamm in the neurology department at the hospital can see him at short notice as a professional favour.'

'What is it that you're afraid of?' she asked, and sat up on her elbow in the bed, suddenly bathed in fear.

'Oh, you know, all the worst things,' he muttered. 'When I'm being sensible, I suspect that all I need is reassurance. It's fine. Of course it is. He was just having a bad day.'

'I'll reassure you, Alec...'

'Will you? The usual way?'

'Maybe the *unusual* way.'

'I like the sound of that.'

And, judging by what followed, he apparently liked the feel of it even more.

In the morning, however, the issue of William's well-being had gone beyond simple reassurance. He couldn't walk. By the time he was admitted to hospital he couldn't move his arms, and by the end of the day he was no longer breathing on his own.

At least they had a tentative diagnosis. Post-infectious polyneuritis, or Guillain-Barré syndrome. They sat in Dr Kamm's office at ten-thirty in the morning and heard it together.

Hot sun came through the windows of the sleek professional building, which was separated from the main hospital building by a car park where shiny vehicles baked in the bright light. Alec leaned forward in his chair, his shoulders hunched and forearms pressed into his thighs, as if in pain.

The neurologist swivelled in his chair every now and then, and twiddled a pen in his fingers.

'It's not at all common in a child of his age,' Dr Kamm told them. 'In fact, it's quite rare. But it can happen, following an upper respiratory illness, or chickenpox, as in this case. We haven't got a definitive diagnosis yet, but everything points to it, and I'm actually quite sure.'

Alec pressed his fingers over his eyes for a moment, then took them away again and said hoarsely, 'Remind me, David. What are the statistics on this?'

'Seventy-five per cent of children will recover completely.'

'And the others?'

A beat of silence.

'I want it straight, David.'

'Percentages?'

'Percentages.'

'Ten to fifteen per cent will have ongoing neurological consequences, some of them serious. A handful more will have minor, insignificant sequelae. Five to seven per cent will die.'

Alec had known this already. Erin could see it in his face, and in the bleak little jerk of his head as he nodded. Erin hadn't known. No, probably *had* known it as a meaningless abstraction. Not the percentages, but the vague fact, retained from study years ago that, yes, on rare occasions a child could contract Guillain-Barré syndrome and die. Today, the bare-faced statistics outlined by Dr Kamm shafted through her like an arrow.

Five to seven per cent. At least one child in twenty.

Not William. *Not* William! Surely now that he was already undergoing treatment, his life wasn't seriously threatened? Was it?

How could Alec bear it? How could she bear it for him? Or for herself?

Only now did she fully realise how strenuously she had

attacked the task of becoming William's mother. She'd changed at least three dozen nappies over the past four weeks, spooned in a hundred mouthfuls of food. She'd played chasey and hidey and peek-a-boo. She'd cut up fruit and toast, read stories, recalled nursery rhymes, made towers with blocks, bought wet wipes and very small socks, got splashed with bath water, and had had her shoulder dampened with tears.

And she'd done it all so willingly, with such hope for her future as Alec's wife and William's stepmother, that now she was caught. She loved William, and love brought pain.

'What happens now?' Alec asked. 'Hell, I *know* this. I should know it! It's not my area. Has anything changed since I last opened a paediatric textbook or walked a children's ward?'

'Of course,' David Kamm said. 'We're getting better at all of this all the time. The basics are the same, though. He's on a gamma globulin drip to boost his immune system so he can fight this strongly and quickly. We monitor his neurological status thoroughly and frequently. We assess his movement and his strength. We check his cranial nerve function. We support his breathing. Put him on a ventilator if necessary, and wean him from it gradually as his respiratory function improves. We monitor his cardiovascular system in case of arrhythmias and hypotension. Abnormal heartbeat and low blood pressure,' he clarified suddenly, for Erin's benefit.

'She's a nurse,' Alec cut in, adding abruptly, 'not his mother.'

'Not William's mother?' Dr Kamm said, with a careful nod.

'No. She's in London. We're divorced,' Alec elaborated, brief to the point of terseness. 'I'll have to phone her.' He didn't expand on the issue, just added, 'What else?'

He didn't look at Erin. Maybe what she felt didn't show on her face, anyway. He hadn't meant to deliver that blow.

How was it a blow? It was a fact! She wasn't William's mother. It didn't change her relationship with Alec, did it?

She shook off the sense of desolation and uncertainty that his words had poured over her. She couldn't let it be important now, in the face of everything else.

'Treatment?' Dr Kamm was saying. 'He'll probably need parenteral or nasogastric feeding. He'll definitely need physiotherapy as soon as the illness begins to resolve. Carefully managed, because some children become very sensitive to touch and movement. Passive and active range-of-motion exercises to start with, moving on to— Well, he'll have to learn to walk again, of course.'

Alec nodded, while Erin thought of William running with her in the park on his chubby little legs, displaying such joy in the simple act of movement. How long would it be before he could do that again? Her breathing came in short, sharp gasps.

'He'll need skin care to prevent pressure sores. And he'll need support, Alec.'

'You don't have to tell me that.'

'No, but I'm telling you anyway. We can't medicate him for pain or distress because anything that depresses his respiration or slows down the recovery of his immune system could be disastrous. So he'll need maximum support from you. And from his mother. If that's possible,' he added. Frowned. Erin knew there would be more questions later on about the family situation.

Dr Kamm looked at her. 'From anyone he's close to,' he revised, and she gave a tiny nod. 'We'll make sure he has particular staff assigned to him consistently, so that changes in his status are recognised as they happen. We'll keep the lines of communication open, Alec. Don't worry about that.'

'I want to get back to him.' Erin heard the barely concealed strain in Alec's voice.

'Of course. I'll come with you and we can talk some more

as we go, if you like.' Dr Kamm rose, and Alec and Erin followed suit.

'When do you think he'll plateau out?' Alec asked.

'We can only wait and see.' He opened the door and ushered them out of the office, through the reception area and waiting room. The place smelled of new carpet. 'The onset has been rapid,' he went on, 'which is good. Usually means it will plateau quickly and ebb quickly as well.'

'What's quickly?' Erin asked. She had to fight to overcome the feeling that she didn't have the right to ask questions, to care this much. She wasn't his mother. Alec had said it himself, taking just four words to get the information across to David Kamm.

They reached the lift and went down one floor.

'Recovery can start within a week or two, from which point measurable improvement happens daily. Given the rapid onset in this case, I'm hoping he'll plateau out within the next few days, possibly with some signs of that within twenty-four hours.'

'He's so little.' Erin's voice broke on the word.

They were crossing the car park now. In the open air, there was a cool, fresh breeze. It wasn't hot, as it had seemed in Dr Kamm's office. Those big panes of glass magnified the sun.

'Don't think of that as all bad,' the neurologist urged them both. 'Yes, this is frightening for him, but a child of his age is very adaptable, and he'll bounce back.'

Seventy-five per cent of the time.

No one said it.

They reached the main building and went up to the high-dependency section of the paediatric intensive care unit, where a highly trained paediatric intensive care nurse had just assessed William's respiratory function once more. The picture revealed by his blood gases and oxygen saturation level was still worsening. Carbon dioxide levels climbing and oxygen falling.

'We'll start respiratory support,' Dr Kamm decreed. 'But we'll hold off on intubation if we can. Just a mask at this stage. Reassess on an ongoing basis. If he develops any difficulty in coughing or swallowing— How's his speech, Alec? Is he talking much?'

'Lots of words. A few two-word sentences.'

'Could you tell if he began to slur his words?'

'I think so, yes.'

The neurologist nodded, then said, 'I have to go, but I'll be back later on.' He picked up William's chart, took a final look at the figures and notations already crowding it, gave Alec's shoulder a brief squeeze and then left.

William looked tiny in his bed. He wasn't outwardly upset, but his eyes never left his father's face over the next hour, and Alec couldn't get him to speak, despite talking to him, singing, telling stories. When William's lunch was brought round, Alec fed it to him in tiny spoonfuls, examining every swallow.

PICU Nurse Martha Johansen worked over him almost constantly, since by the time she had assessed and noted the full set of functions and indicators, it was time to go back to the beginning again. She was a big-boned woman in her forties with threads of grey in her dark hair, a very plain face, a musical voice and an incredibly wide, beautiful smile.

'That's all right, honey-pie, just popping this silly thing around your arm again. Doesn't hurt, does it? Tickles, then feels a bit tight.'

Erin would have understood what Martha was doing if she had paid attention to it, but she didn't. Couldn't. Had no room in her mind for all that right now. Her gaze and her focus were both locked onto William and Alec, and she was trying in a hazy, uncertain way to get to know Martha as well.

Do I trust her? Do I like her? Is she doing it all right? Does she care about William?

Finally, at about one, he fell into a light sleep, an oxygen mask over his little face.

'You need to eat, Alec,' Erin told him gently. 'We both do.'

'What? Oh. No, I...' He blinked.

'Take the chance now,' she urged. 'You won't want to leave him when he wakes again.'

'I'm not hungry.'

'Still, you have to eat.' She could see his irritation mounting, but pressed on anyway, churned up and stubborn. 'What happens if *you* get sick? You have to look after yourself. This is going to go on for weeks.'

'OK. You're right.' He didn't apologise, but it didn't matter. He gripped her hand briefly instead, then pressed his hands to his face as if working the muscles loose. After a moment, he went on in a determined tone, 'First, though, I want to see about getting time off work. Till the end of next week, if I possibly can. I'm not going to leave him alone. Not for one waking minute, when he doesn't understand all this. God!' He gave a dry sob. 'This must be so frightening for him!'

'I'm here, too. I can be with him. Alison—'

'Yes, but I'm his father. What time is it in London?'

The two sentences, hard on top of one another with no obvious connection, sent an icy dart through Erin, but she didn't let it show. Calculated rapidly instead. She was filled with a painful need to be helpful. At this time of year, early April... England had daylight saving, which had ended in Australia at the end of last month... London was nine hours behind. 'Four-thirty in the morning,' she said.

'I don't care. I'm going to phone her.'

Kate.

'Yes, of course. You must,' she agreed.

'Meet me in the cafeteria?' he suggested. 'Order me something. Don't care what it is. Soup, or something.'

'More than that, Alec.'

He waved this aside. 'I don't care. Now, where can I phone from?'

He strode from the unit without another word, not having expected an answer to that question about where to find a phone.

Erin slumped back into a chair beside William's high, elaborate bed and watched him for a few minutes. He looked so tiny. So still.

'Complicated,' Martha commented out of the silence.

Erin stirred herself. 'Oh... Yes.' And because she knew that William's medical and nursing staff would need to understand the situation, she sketched it out. 'Alec is divorced. Alec and I are...' She hesitated. 'Engaged. Kate, his ex-wife, William's mother, is in London. She's Kate Gilchrist. The actress. You might have seen her recently in... Oh, Lord, what's it called? My mind's gone blank. That film with the whole time travel element, with the guy from—'

'Sorry, I...' Martha smiled apologetically and shook her head.

'Doesn't matter.' Hell, of course it doesn't! 'She had a supporting role. She's good in it, apparently.'

Rachel had seen the film, and had reported back on it last week. Alec hadn't mentioned it, and Erin hadn't suggested going.

'So she'll fly out?'

'I don't know.'

'Surely—'

'Yes. Yes, of course she will.'

Silence.

'Go and get your lunch, hey?' Martha reminded her gently.

Erin roused herself and went down to the cafeteria, collected two huge hot lunches as if they were on a programme to gain weight. She didn't want to start until Alec arrived, so she bustled about collecting extra plates to put over the dishes to keep them hot. She knew she was behaving illogically but couldn't manage to stop.

He arrived fifteen minutes after she had sat down at the table.

'She's coming, and I've got the time off.' He sounded breathless, relieved, shaky. Gripped her hands for a moment, then let them go. He felt ice cold. 'Brian was great about it. They'll arrange cover. Ling Farrow says she doesn't mind doing more hours.' His eyes looked glazed and distant. 'Kate's going to leave a message on the machine at home with her flight details as soon as she knows them.'

He lapsed into silence and sat down, watching while Erin removed all her dish covers. 'Cutlery. Cups. Tea,' she said pointlessly, setting it all out.

'What's all this?'

'Lunch.'

'For a horse.'

'No, horses eat hay,' she retorted.

'I can't eat this!' His tone was harsh and impatient.

'Neither can I. Do you think *I'm* hungry? My God, Alec!' Her voice cracked. 'I'm not trying to torture you with food for my own pleasure.'

'Erin. Oh…Erin.' He pressed her hand, chafed it. 'I'm sorry. Let's start again. Thanks for getting lunch. I'll do my best with it.'

'I'm sorry, too,' she said, then confessed abruptly, from the heart, 'I'm not looking forward to seeing Kate. I don't know…where she'll fit in. Where *I'll* fit in. And how I'll handle it.' She felt sick at having put it into words. Her fears only seemed more real now.

'We'll manage,' he assured her automatically.

She sensed he'd hardly taken in the meaning of her words. It wasn't the right moment to have said it all. Still, he half

stood, stretched his hard, warm body across the table and
kissed her, sweeping his lids closed, parting his mouth softly,
tasting her, clinging for a moment, letting go. As he sat back,
she saw that the front tail of his shirt had come untucked on
one side and dipped its hem into the soup, but this didn't
seem to matter.

They looked at each other helplessly, started spooning in
the soup, stopped again.

Then he said the words she had known were coming for
at least four hours now.

'We'll have to cancel the wedding.'

CHAPTER FIVE

ERIN nodded at Alec. 'I know.'

He didn't add anything more. No apologies or reasoning, nothing about rescheduling when they had time to think about it. Since she hadn't expected anything like this, and understood exactly how he was feeling, why he couldn't think that far ahead, she didn't dwell on it. Of course they'd reschedule it, when there was enough room in their minds to think about such things.

'Mel's already on the plane,' she said instead.

'Is she? Yes, she would be, wouldn't she?'

'My shift starts at three. It's two now. I'll probably just have time to drop past Rachel's and ask if she can phone everyone else for us. The caterers. The celebrant. The hotel. Family, of course.'

'How will she know who to call?'

'Oh, I have this little notebook. I— You see, I bought a— a bridal magazine a couple of weeks ago—' to be strictly honest, three bride magazines '—and it suggested that it was a good idea to keep…'

She stopped. It seemed too trivial even to explain, and she'd never told Alec about the bridal magazines before. Hadn't brought them to his place. They were sitting on her coffee-table at home, in a little pile that said 'impulse purchase'. It was something she had felt slightly guilty about, especially when she'd actually taken the magazine's *advice* and started that 'wedding planner' notebook.

Bridal magazines were for women who had their weddings planned months in advance, as Kate had, with dozens of guests and hundreds of details.

Still, the fact remained, she'd started the notebook and it had all the phone numbers and contact details relating to the event. Under the circumstances, this was a piece of good fortune, when good fortune was decidedly thin on the ground at the moment.

Alec hadn't queried her uncompleted sentence. He was doggedly forking in his hot lunch of chicken casserole, rice and vegetables, with gulps of tea in between. He would return to William as soon as he finished. He seemed to have turned in on himself. She didn't know what he was thinking, suspected it was the same things over and over, running around his head like a mouse on one of those wheels.

Erin did her best with her own meal, and they put down their forks at the same time.

'If I can take a break during my shift,' she said as she rose, 'I'll come…'

'Yes, do come up.' He nodded. 'Please!'

He took both her hands in his and squeezed them, pressed his cheek against hers. It felt warm and rough and she wanted to cover it, cover his whole face, with fervent kisses.

'Where's Kate going to stay?' she blurted.

He blinked and grimaced, as if the problem were too hard even to grasp, let alone solve. 'We'll deal with that later. A hotel, or something.' He waved the issue aside like an irritating fly. 'You'd better get going if you want to catch Rachel.'

'Mmm.'

He left without clearing his plate, so she did it for him. Another pointless task for her hands. You were supposed to clear away your own things, but if you didn't, the cafeteria staff came and did it for you.

At home, she grabbed the jaunty little notebook and changed into her uniform, in and out the door in five minutes. Rachel was weeding in the front garden, while Archie took his nap.

'Hi!' she said cheerfully, pulling off her gardening gloves and shading her eyes with the back of her hand. 'Got time for a cuppa?'

Erin answered with a sob and got a hug which she fought off. 'I have to be at work in ten minutes,' she said.

'What's wrong?'

'William…has Guillain-Barré syndrome—and—'

'What's that?'

'It's an auto-immune— They think it's a—' She waved her hands, gulped, cut to the heart of it. 'He should survive. He shouldn't die. But it hasn't plateaued yet. That's the critical thing, apparently—one of them—the point at which it plateaus out. It's looking like he'll probably go on a ventilator. Kate's flying out. We're cancelling the wedding. Here's the book. Can you phone everyone and tell them?'

'Erin—!'

'I can't stop. I can't talk about it. I don't want questions or opinions, Rachel.'

'No. No, of course you don't,' her sister-in-law said quietly. 'Don't worry. I'll handle everything. Phone with news when you can.'

Erin nodded, jumped back in the car, drove around the corner and was so shaky that she had to stop for several minutes at the side of the street until she could continue safely.

They intubated William and put him on a ventilator at four o'clock that afternoon. Erin wasn't there to see it, but Alec told her about it when she managed to get up to the PICU during her meal break, and she knew it would have been ghastly for him to watch. Harder, perhaps, than it had been for William to experience.

Alec already looked exhausted, as if he'd missed a night's sleep, and she didn't know how she was going to get him to take proper care of himself. Didn't feel as if she had the authority to insist, to cajole, to do it for him. There was a distance in his eyes that she didn't want to challenge, and their love was too new. Ridiculous, when she'd loved him for four years, but there it was. Their love was still too new.

'When are you going to take a break, Alec?' That was all she dared to say at first.

He shrugged.

He was holding William's hand. The little boy was awake, lost amongst tubes and monitors. With the tube down his throat, he could no longer speak, or cry audibly. He was being fed by tube now, and still had a drip in his arm as well. Two drips, in fact. He might have fought all this equipment, only none of his muscles could move. Even his darling little smile was gone.

'How about if I stay with him overnight?' she persisted.

'I want to wait until it looks like he's plateaued out. David is hoping there'll be evidence of that overnight. Oh…' He shook his head. 'You were there, of course, when he said it.'

She nodded. 'OK.'

'Will you meet Mel at the airport tomorrow?' he asked.

'I've forgotten her flight time.'

'Eight forty-five.'

'What airline?'

'Can't remember. The information is by the phone. I think. In that little drawer in the phone table. I'm pretty sure.'

'I'll find it.'

'Are you staying the night?' he asked.

'I thought you said—'

'Not here. At my place.'

'I hadn't—'

'Can you, please?' He looked at her properly for just a moment. 'In case Kate phones?'

'Of course.'

'Find out what she wants to do about accommodation. Offer her the study.' He was looking at William again now.

'The study.' She nodded.

Didn't plague him with the issue of where she would be staying herself. Not with Kate in Alec's house. Back at her own place, then.

She took a deep, jerky breath.

'Is it OK if I kiss him, Alec?' she asked.

'Oh, Lord, of course it is!' He did another one of those blink-and-wake-up-for-a-moment things that she was starting to recognise. 'Kiss me, too, while you're at it,' he growled. Then added belatedly, 'Please!'

So they kissed. The tears on Erin's lashes transferred themselves to his cheeks. He must have felt the tiny droplets of moisture because he pulled back a little, looked at her and stroked the hair back from her forehead.

'Can't imagine what this would be like without you,' he said, but his voice was stiff, creaky with effort. 'You're the only star in the sky for me right now. Forgive…everything, can you?'

'Nothing to forgive, Alec,' she whispered, then turned, bent down and rested her lips on William's forehead for a moment. 'Hang in there, little one,' she told him softly, and left him alone with Alec once more.

Alec opened his eyes and stretched in a vain attempt to loosen his knotted muscles. The vertebrae in his neck burned, the long muscle beneath his ear was stretched and aching, and one of his legs had gone numb.

Lord, what was the time? He looked at the numbers on the ventilator. 1.35. He'd been asleep, then. Not intentionally, and not for long. About twenty minutes. Less, probably. Just enough to induce this stiffness and chill and disorientation, but not enough to refresh him in the slightest.

He caught a movement at the edge of his vision and saw the night nurse, Barbara O'Shaunessy, tiptoe in to make her regular series of checks on William. He sat up straighter, suddenly alert and bathed in panic. Hell, how could sleep have overtaken him like that, even for a moment?

'How is he?' His voice cracked and caught in his throat, barely audible. He cleared it impatiently. 'How is he doing?'

He stood, didn't care if he was getting in trimly built Barbara's way. She could deal with it. He wanted to see for himself what was going on. She stepped aside to accommodate him, and went through it all patiently.

Blood pressure, temperature and pulse. Heart rhythm. Oxygen saturation. Reflex responses. Urinary output.

'No change…no worsening…in the past two hours, Dr Rostrevor.'

'That's great. That's good.'

Weak with relief, he sank back into the chair and took William's limp hand. Two sleepy eyes opened and looked at him steadily, imprisoned in the small, motionless body. 'It's all right, William, Daddy's here,' he whispered. 'Go back to sleep, little boy.'

The eyes closed again.

Behind him, Alec sensed movement and felt a soft, familiar hand on his shoulder.

'Did he wake up?'

He twisted around. 'Erin, I thought you must have gone home.'

'Of course not,' she said, managing a smile for him. 'Just to make some tea. Came to ask if you want some.'

'I've drunk about five litres of the stuff tonight!' he answered. 'But, sure, go ahead. Bring me some tea if you want.'

She nodded and turned, and he almost called her back, feeling that once again he'd been too offhand and abrupt with her, not appreciative enough of her care. It was radiating at him like a fully fired up furnace, steady and glowing and hot, and his heart moved strangely in his chest at the thought of her love.

She didn't know what she was getting herself into. Dear Lord, she had no idea!

It wasn't the first time he'd thought this, but the strength of his conviction on the subject was growing by quantum leaps. He hated the fact that he was dragging her through this, and that he was so shamelessly greedy for the support she could give.

A few minutes later, she returned with his tea in a thick, sturdy mug. Just the way he liked it, medium strength with a little bit of milk. She always got it right.

Sitting in another chair a little more distant from William's bed, she sipped her own brew several times in silence, then gave him a momentary half-smile. He returned it, but couldn't speak, couldn't think of the right thing to say.

Thank you. I love you. Forgive me. Go away.

So he turned to watch William and hoped she couldn't know how much his thoughts were churning over her.

Had it been an act of pure selfishness, rather than pure love, coming out here to claim her the way he had? he wondered.

On the surface, it didn't seem that way. He was the one who'd made the running, who'd uprooted his life. That spoke of love, didn't it, not selfishness? Erin herself saw it in those terms, he knew. Caitlin, her sister, had been right on that score.

When they'd spoken by phone, months ago, she'd insisted, 'Erin needs to see that you mean it. Actions, not words. Don't just fly out here for a couple of weeks and expect her to go back with you. If you mean it, if you love her, come out here to live. Set yourself up before you even make contact, so that she can't send you packing even if she says she wants to.'

The idea had held an enormous and surprisingly seductive appeal. What he'd loved in Erin Gray from the beginning, before he'd ever realised it, had been the aura of sunshine

and openness that she'd brought with her, the antithesis of
Kate's studied grace and good manners.

Erin didn't have to practise her warmth or cultivate her
passion. They spilled out of her instinctively. She never hung
back, was always willing to laugh, to love, to give. Perhaps
that was what Caitlin had been trying to protect in her older
sister—Erin's tendency to give, before she'd even been
asked.

Caitlin had rightly wanted the sacrifices to work both
ways.

Not, actually, that deciding to make his life here had been
a sacrifice. He had liked Australia the moment he'd set foot
on its soil, and he still did. He liked the refreshing honesty
of many of its people, their rough good humour, their lack
of pretension. He liked Canberra's crispy, sunny weather. He
liked the blue skies and the baroque carolling of the black,
golden-eyed currawong birds in the trees. He liked the way
the pointed leaves of the eucalypts hung in the air and the
graceful curves of their warm, pale trunks against the sky.

He felt free here, in a way he'd never felt in England—
broken free of the bonds of tradition and family, the cold
pettiness of his parents' determination to remind him how
often he'd been a disappointment to them. That brief, ludicrous foray into an arty career, which they still brought up
in tones of distaste and embarrassment, and now his crassness
in preferring some silly little Australian nurse to perfect
Kate... Well, *really*!

And, by all that was holy, it had been good not to have to
consider Kate any more, to know instead that she was half a
world away, out of his life. Out of *William's* life, so that
Alec didn't have to worry about the effect of her erratic,
selfish love on a child's tender heart.

He let out a sigh, controlling it at the last second as he
became aware of Erin, still patiently and quietly sitting, sharing his vigil. His stomach churned with guilt about what he

would be putting her through over the coming weeks. What he'd already put her through since they'd met.

Kate was probably packing at this very moment, and would be leaving for the airport within a few hours. She wasn't going to be half a world away any more. And she had been distraught on the phone, shocked out of her former complacency that things had worked out for the best.

'My God, and I just let you do it, didn't I?' she had sobbed. 'I let you take him away, because of that trivial girl, so that now he's at the God-forsaken end of the earth, his life is in danger, and I can't be with him. I must have been crazy!'

What have I done? he though bleakly. What have I so blithely asked Erin to do? Marry me, become William's mother when he has a mother already. How much have I really been considering Erin's needs?

I conned myself into thinking that coming out here was the grand gesture of compromise and sacrifice. But it wasn't. I bulldozed her into those wedding arrangements, ignored the disappointment in her, even though I could see it, when I let myself. She thought she'd hidden it, but she hadn't.

I didn't give her time to pause for breath. Well, now there's no choice.

It was a bitter realisation.

Erin would have plenty of time. And plenty of opportunity to realise just how much he had been asking of her, just how much more there was to all this than their blithe and hungry confessions of love. What if she started to look at what she felt in a whole new way?

Again, the roil of panic and rebellion that he felt at this thought seemed like pure selfishness, and he wondered suddenly, Are Kate and I two of a kind after all? Perhaps we deserve each other, belong together in a horrible, upside-down sort of a way. Hell, wouldn't that be ironic?

'It's all right, love, it's all right.'

Erin's voice.

For a moment, he thought she was talking to him. He stirred his throat ready to say, Thanks, yes, I know it is, because you're here. Then he realised it was William she was talking to.

He had awoken again, and silent tears were running down his little cheeks. Erin was holding his hand and stroking it. She began to sing, and Alec lunged out of his seat and leant over the bed as well.

'We're both here, little man,' he said, his voice choking. Then he let Erin soothe William…and himself…with her sweet, quiet lullaby.

'Erin!'

Mel Rostrevor lunged out of a crowd of business travellers and into Erin's arms at Canberra airport the next morning. She hadn't changed much in two years. Still petite, dark-haired and vibrant, with two wicked dimples at the corners of her mouth when she smiled, and roving brown eyes which proclaimed her always ready for a laugh or an escapade.

She was viewing this trip to Australia and tomorrow's wedding—tomorrow's *cancelled* wedding—as escapades, Erin could tell at once.

'Oh, Mel, it's good to see you!' she said, her voice all over the place.

'That flight's murderous, isn't it?' Mel groaned.

'Yes. Horrible. Endless.'

'And so noisy! How do I look? Shopping bags under my eyes, yeah? Eagles nesting in my hair?'

'All of that,' Erin agreed, with a hiccup of strained laughter.

Mel hasn't noticed yet that anything is wrong, she thought. She's too bubbly and happy to be here. How do I tell her? I don't want to tell her at all. It's such a relief to pretend for thirty seconds that everything's fine, that I'm marrying her brother tomorrow and that she and I are as silly and frivolous together as we ever were.

But thirty seconds was as long as it lasted. Silly and frivolous Mel might be on occasion, but she had a warm heart and a perceptive mind.

'Erin?' Already she had stiffened doubtfully, pulled back at arm's length and begun to search her friend's face. 'Is there something…?'

'William is ill. Kate's coming out. We've cancelled the wedding.'

Mel paled and clutched Erin's arms. 'How ill?'

'Guillain-Barré syndrome. He's on a ventilator. At least—now—they're pretty sure he'll live.'

'Oh, my Lord!'

They stood out of the way of the foot traffic at the top of the escalator which descended to the exit and baggage claim area and talked about it, heedless of the passengers still trooping past.

Erin had last seen Alec and William at four in the morning, after she'd stayed on at the hospital following the end of her shift. William's condition had appeared to be stable. It was possible that he'd reached the plateau that was so important, and he had been sleeping. Erin had brought Alec some supper at about two-thirty, yet another cup of tea and the biscuits that were available in the unit, as well as a packet of lurid orange corn chips from a vending machine down near the hospital gift shop.

He had eaten and drunk these offerings dutifully and silently. They'd sat together for a further hour and a half, tired, stiff, silent, strained. Occasionally, he'd taken her hand and given it a squeeze. Mostly he hadn't even done that. He'd folded his arms across his chest as if he hadn't wanted to touch her, and she'd felt helpless, useless. Perhaps he'd have preferred to have been alone, but she'd had to trust that her presence had been of some value.

He'd told her several times to go home. She hadn't budged until he'd finally fallen asleep once more himself, sprawled uncomfortably in the chair by the bed.

His cheek had been pillowed on one shoulder, his arms folded across his stomach and one leg had been half tucked beneath him, probably going numb. She'd wanted to kiss him, wallpaper his entire face with the imprint of her mouth, brush a stray biscuit crumb from his face as well, but had been too afraid of waking him. Instead, she'd tiptoed out to a nurse and asked for a blanket, which she'd draped lightly over him. It had seemed like such a tiny gesture.

He would be awake again by now, and probably feeling about a hundred years old.

'Can I go straight to the hospital?' Mel wanted to know.

The crowd of departing passengers had dwindled to a trickle then petered out altogether. Now the flight crew was leaving as well. Canberra wasn't a big airport. It might be some minutes before another flight came in. The escalator rolled with a mechanical rattle, empty. Mel and Erin started down to the ground floor.

'If you're not too tired,' Erin answered her friend.

'Course I'm not. Wouldn't sleep.'

'No.' Erin herself had spent just a few restless, useless hours in bed. Couldn't envisage, at the moment, when she'd next be likely to enjoy a good night. 'I want to get back to the hospital as well, so we'll set you up later at—'

She stopped. Alec had suggested that Kate use the study-cum-spare-room at his place. There had been a well-controlled, clearly enunciated message from her on the answering machine when Erin had checked it this morning. She had made all her travel arrangements, and she would be on the same flight into Canberra that Mel had just taken, arriving at eight forty-five tomorrow morning.

'At Alec's,' Erin finished, remembering that there was a single bed in William's room.

'OK,' Mel agreed, not very interested in the accommodation issue.

They had arrived at the baggage claim area. She pulled a
soft suitcase off the moving belt. 'This is it.'

'Travelling light.'

'With plans for major shopping. Oh, but, hell, not any
more!'

Erin gave a dry sob in reply.

'Where's Kate staying?' Mel asked, after a moment. They
were on their way to the car.

'Alec's. Well, he'll offer that when she gets here.'

'Oh, no! Uh-uh! In that case, I am *not* staying at Alec's!'

'Mel—'

'Listen, if I want to see a one-woman show, I go to the
theatre. Is that petty, when things are so dire? I don't care,
Erin! I will *not* be able to stand by and watch Kate giving
whatever beautiful, heart-rending performance she considers
appropriate for this occasion! I don't know why Alec could
never see it—'

'I think he could see it,' Erin said. 'Quite clearly. I think
he felt…knew…that there was more underneath.' Was she
defending Alec or Kate?

'Will *you* be able to stand it? All of us under the same
roof?'

'I…won't be,' Erin answered. 'Under the same roof, I
mean. I'll be back at my place.'

Was she just running away, though? Treating her little
town house with its mercifully unexpired lease as a bolthole?

No, it was more than that…*worse* than that. It was a rec-
ognition on her part that what had happened—William's illness—wasn't just a temporary hiccup in her life. No matter
what happened to him—her mind swerved away from the
worst scenario, which was mercifully less likely now, but her
heart tore a little more anyway—the balance in the complex

web of relationships that surrounded and involved her had irrevocably changed.

Mel said, 'Then I'll stay with you.' Silence, followed by a short 'Oh!' of realisation. 'Actually, no, I won't,' she amended quickly. 'I *will* stay at Alec's after all.'

'But you said—'

They reached Erin's car.

'Doesn't matter. Have to be bigger than that, don't I? More generous.'

'Generous?' Erin laughed shakily. 'You could generously give me the comfort of your company at my place. I'd like that. I hadn't expected to be using it after tonight, and it feels pretty barren.'

'I'll stay at Alec's,' Mel insisted, then blurted, 'Lord, Erin, you don't really think I'm going to leave Alec and Kate alone together every night, do you? In view of what's going on? I'm sorry, but when our darling little guy is well again and there's another wedding in the works, I want *you* to be the bride, not Kate!' She saw Erin's face. 'Oh, hell, I shouldn't have said that!'

Erin sat at the wheel of her car, not moving. 'I'm sorry, can't drive yet,' she gasped.

'No, *I'm* sorry. Of course you can't. I'm so sorry. And I'm wrong. There's no danger. He doesn't love Kate.'

'But you said—'

'Wasn't thinking.' Her arms came around Erin's shoulders. 'Just shoot me, could you? Send me to a hotel. In Perth.'

'You *said* it, Mel. At some level, you think—'

'Lord, I have to address this, don't I?' She took a deep breath. 'I suppose…I've seen a lot of emotion over children, especially ill children. Drives some couples apart.'

'Brings others together again,' Erin finished. 'I've seen it, too.'

'Yes. It does.' She shrugged. It was another apology. 'And Kate is…unpredictable in her needs and desires.'

'Is Alec, though?'

'No. He's not. Of course you're right. It takes two, doesn't it?'

'That's the usual idea.'

'I can't imagine that she could grow that much, change that much, even with something like this as a trigger. And I can't imagine he'd respond if she did. Not now…when there's you.'

'No,' Erin agreed obediently. But she began to wonder. For William's sake, especially now, was there anything that Alec wouldn't do?

'Still, I'll stay with Alec,' Mel concluded firmly. '*Not* for that reason, Erin! But he'll need support.'

'He'll have Kate. The mother of his child. And me. It's not as if I'll be out of the picture.'

'Of course not.' Mel shook her head and gave a little scream of frustration at the complexity of it. 'Look, how about I plan to stay at Alec's for the moment and we'll reassess when we've talked to him? How can any of us make rational decisions at a time like this?'

'Give me another minute, OK, before we go?'

'As long as you like, sweetie.' Mel patted her helplessly again.

'Tell me some gossip, Mel,' Erin begged. 'Some big, fat gossip from London, dripping with juice and scandal, about people I've never met.'

'Gossip. Oh, gossip! Well, I've always got that…' She launched into an elaborate story, and by the time it was finished Erin was able to drive.

They arrived at the hospital within twenty minutes of leaving the airport.

Alec stood up at once when he saw Mel, so stiff you could practically hear him creak.

He wasn't interested in greetings or platitudes, just cut straight to a rambling, painful report, his face closed and pale.

Erin ached for him. Felt paralysed. Like William was. Powerless to *do* anything for this man she loved so freshly and so painfully.

'He's awake,' Alec began. 'Stable. Teary. So still, though. I— Little children don't usually cry quietly. It's unbearable! Never knew…how much I could long for those loud, red-faced, stormy shrieks of his when I take him away from something he wants. You know how they cry with their whole bodies at this age?'

He managed a smile, but then it broke and he covered his face with his hands, pressed his fingers deeply into his tired skin. Erin went up to him and held him. Selfish of her, probably. Mel must have wanted a hug from her brother. Mel would just have to wait!

She felt him shudder in her arms. She had brought his toothbrush, a change of clothing, some pieces of fruit, even his hairbrush and razor. Each item, packed into a small overnight bag, said, I love you, but perhaps she was the only one who could hear the words.

The three of them spent the next hour at William's bedside, one of those disorganised sequences of time in which no one said anything in the right order, no one answered each other's questions properly.

They couldn't tell if William remembered Mel. It was almost two months since he had seen her. She studied his chart, passed it to Erin, got Alec to explain anything she didn't understand. It gave them all something to talk about.

'So he's possibly, *probably* plateaued,' Mel summarised. 'And the worst danger has passed.'

'We can't drop our guard, though,' Alec said. 'He's still more vulnerable to all sorts of problems. His immune system is barely functioning, and we have to hope that the gamma globulin will strengthen it quickly.'

'How long before he starts to recover some movement?'

'A week or two,' Alec answered. 'It'll ease pretty much

in the reverse order to how it began. He'll start intensive physiotherapy within the next couple of days. He should regain the ability to breathe on his own first. I keep thinking that if it had plateaued just a little sooner, he'd at least have been spared that.'

He indicated the ventilator with its quiet, ceaselessly rhythmic hiss, and the tube down William's throat which meant that he could neither talk nor cry.

'A week or two of this? Then weeks more of gradual recovery? It's going to be bloody boring, isn't it?' Mel said lightly.

It sounded like a harsh comment, but Alec understood.

'Yes,' he said. 'Odd combination, really. Emotional agony coupled with tedium.' He laughed. 'Hell, you have to poke fun at it, don't you? I'm a mess, Mel, if you haven't noticed.'

'Got a few clues,' she said.

William fell asleep and she insisted that Alec and Erin leave the hospital for a while. They did. They went to Alec's, and discovered they'd left his overnight bag at the hospital. So much for Erin's careful, love-filled packing! Now he couldn't shave.

'Not that I care,' he said, and didn't add any thanks to her for packing the things in the first place. She shrugged it off. 'What shall we do?' he added vaguely.

'Eat, then sleep,' she suggested. Wanted to say, Talk, but knew it would be wrong.

So they made tea and grilled cheese and tomato on toast. He switched on the radio and it burbled away in the background with a news bulletin that neither of them cared about. Erin switched it off again when Alec went to the bathroom and he didn't even notice.

They folded themselves into bed at the unsettling hour of eleven forty-five in the morning. Erin didn't expect anything to happen. Sleep? Perhaps not even that. Perhaps they'd both be too tense. As for the other…

But when he cradled her from behind, beneath the covers, buried his face in her hair and simply said her name, she turned to him, kissed every inch of his face with passionate tenderness and they did end up making love, with no words spoken at all.

Erin hardly dared to look at his face as he pulled hungrily at her underclothes. His eyes were narrowed and glittering, then when they were both naked he closed them. Normally it was a sight she loved, those creamy lids and lashes so silky and black they looked as if they were painted onto his cheeks with a sable brush. Today, though, they seemed to shut her out.

Even his kisses shut her out. His hands were too desperate on her body, and the rhythmic thrust of his hips against her inner thighs was too impatient. Their shared climax was as jagged and tumultuous and earth-shattering as ever, but it didn't seem like a communication or a precious gift to each other today, the way it always had before.

She felt as if she was locked away in her own body, capable only of physical not emotional release, and he was clearly feeling the same. Perhaps, under the circumstances, it had to be that way, but the feeling was raw and imperfect nevertheless. Not his fault. Not hers. Just deeply sad.

Once sated, he fell asleep immediately, overtaken by his exhaustion. He needed it so badly that she couldn't wish he'd stayed awake, so she held him until she slept, too, trying not to disturb him with her shuddering when she cried.

Later on, they went to the hospital separately.

Alec left first, while Erin, not working that day, stayed and tidied the house to an obsessive degree, then rang Alison with an update on William's condition. On the way to the hospital, she stopped at Rachel's. She'd phoned her sister-in-law from the PICU last night with a progress report for Rachel to relay to the rest of the family, but felt out of touch and guilty at the brevity of the conversation.

She hadn't even remembered to thank Rachel for all the phone calls she had already made, or to check whether there was anyone Rachel had been unable to reach.

Rachel met her at the door with a tearful Archie, who had just woken from his nap, and Erin's heart did what felt like a triple back somersault at the contrast between this little boy and Alec's. As he himself had said that morning, there was something intensely reassuring about the vigour of a healthy child's cry.

'Come in,' Rachel said above the noise, and Erin accepted the offer of tea.

Before the kettle had even boiled, Rachel betrayed a characteristic ability to cut to the heart of difficult issues.

'Listen, I've been thinking,' she said, then interrupted herself twice in quick succession. It was a motherly talent that Erin had begun to acquire as well. Maybe she'd lose it again now. She didn't know when she'd next need it again. 'Archie, not in your mouth, love. Do you want Earl Grey?'

'Lovely.'

'Where's Kate staying?'

'Alec's.'

'Yes... Make it my place. Much better idea, don't you think?'

'Rachel, you've never even met her!'

'Irrelevant. *Not* in your mouth, Archie. It's not *who* she is, Erin, it's *what* she is. The ex-wife. She can't stay at Alec's.'

Erin cracked.

'Why is *everybody* convinced—' her voice rose '—that my...' She paused, then selected the most unflattering word she could find. 'My *hold* over Alec is so tenuous that a few nights under the same roof with his ex-wife will be enough to have him walking off into the sunset with her?'

'But it's not going to be a few nights, Erin,' Rachel pointed out gently. 'It's going to be weeks, isn't it?'

'Weeks...'

Weeks.

'And, anyway, I wasn't thinking of that. My goodness, of course I wasn't! I was actually thinking the reverse. That they'd be at each other's throats.'

'Oh, bless you, Rachel!' Erin exclaimed shakily.

'Why, who's been suggesting the other thing?'

'Me. Mainly me. Well, and Mel, but the real fear is coming from me.'

'Silly!'

'Last time I saw the two of them together—' her voice began to fog '—they were in the middle of this picture-perfect wedding. Hard to get that image out of my head, despite everything that's happened since. And they have a child together, a child who is gravely ill. That's, like, the *mother* of emotional connections, isn't it?'

Rachel nodded slowly. 'Yes, that makes sense. You poor thing. Drink that.' She slid the steaming mug of tea across, and they covered quite a bit more necessary conversational ground as they each drank.

There was an update on the cancelled wedding. Erin's parents were still coming up to visit William, but Caitlin and Angus had cried off. Caitlin wasn't well. 'Some kind of flu,' Angus had said yesterday.

'Pregnant.' That was Rachel's opinion. 'Definitely. Doesn't want to say anything yet. Taking it easy. Sick as a dog and knows we'd all guess.'

Erin had to agree that it sounded like a plausible theory, and hoped very much, with the small amount of emotional energy she had to spare, that it was true. Twenty minutes later, she was on her way back to the hospital.

Erin awoke on the morning of what should have been her wedding day with a stiff neck, stale clothes, a headache and tired eyes.

She knew at once where she was. William's bedside. She had finally persuaded Alec to leave the hospital at about midnight, after he'd taken just one hour off earlier in the evening to take Mel for a quick Thai meal.

It hadn't been much of a welcome for his sister. Jet-lagged, she had been ready for bed early, and he'd driven her back to his place, collected her suitcase once more and taken it and Mel herself to Erin's. With Rachel insistent that Kate would be well cared for at her place, Mel was now prepared to abandon her role as chaperone. Alec, they all knew, would hardly be home so it made little sense for anyone to stay with him.

'Why don't you stay at my place, tonight, too?' Erin had suggested to him. 'Someone to talk to when she wakes up in the morning.'

He had agreed it was a good idea, and she was pleased, too, that he'd felt William would be comforted by her presence when he awoke during the night. Now the little boy was still sleeping. He was doing a lot of that, which was good.

Erin went to the bathroom to splash her face and freshen up, then returned to find Martha Johansen working over him. She attached a fresh bag of fluid to his drip, adjusted his position in bed and propped him with pillows, took his routine observations and noted them down.

And then, a good fifteen minutes before Erin had begun to expect them, Alec and Kate appeared.

They must have come straight from the airport. Alec looked a little refreshed after a reasonable night's sleep, although he was hauntingly pale, with blue shadows beneath his eyes. He wore casual clothes—dark denim jeans and an open-necked knit shirt in pale grey. There was something different about him, though. A habitual reserve, which Erin hadn't seen for a while, was locked back into place in his body. His emotions—whatever they were—were simmering quietly, held in check behind a mask of courtesy and coping.

Kate Gilchrist inevitably made a far more vivid impact. She stood in the doorway for a moment, as if frightened to enter, and glanced like a nervous, skittish colt at the other three high-dependency beds and their small occupants, divided from each other by floor-to-ceiling partitions. Alec's hand was hovering around the small of her back and finally rested there. Supporting her? Pushing her forward? Caressing her? Erin couldn't tell.

Kate's dark, figure-hugging clothes emphasised both her slender build and her vibrant colouring. Glossy, red-gold hair, shimmering brown eyes. She looked absurdly innocent and youthful for her thirty-two years.

She was pale, though. Erin thought at first that she wasn't wearing any make-up at all, but, in fact, there were traces of artificial colour around her eyes and a transparent gloss expertly applied to her lips. She grabbed Alec's upper sleeve tightly, stretching the fabric across his biceps, not looking at him but leaning a good part of her weight on him as if he were a post. His hand still rested on her back, a little higher now.

At last she let go and came forward, her eyes fixed on the bed. 'Is this him?' she whispered. 'Oh, it is! Oh, my William!'

She ignored Erin utterly, apart from one careless flick of her gaze, then knelt by the bed, reached out her hand and touched him gently and gracefully on the cheek. Erin sat stiffly in the chair, her body burning, feeling as awkward and out of place in this scene as a large marble sculpture.

'Help me, Alec, I don't know what to do!' Kate said, and her voice cracked musically.

'Talk to him, that's all,' Alec said. 'Don't touch him too much.'

'Don't...?' She looked up at him, her brows lightly furrowed. Her whole face was still saying, Help me! The silent

appeal of the expression etched her features so that she could
have been a Madonna in a Renaissance painting.

'We've had some indications that he's very sensitive to it
at the moment,' Alec explained, as if it was a huge effort.
He came forward, his eyes locked on his son and his son's
mother. 'That it can actually hurt him. It's a recognised
symptom. Fortunately, he's managing to sleep a lot. Looks
like he might drift off in a few minutes.'

'I can see that…'

'Don't expect much of a response of any kind, because he
can barely move a muscle.'

She shook her head mutely, her eyes very large. 'He's
grown so much.'

'Of course. It's been four months, Kate. You were out of
the country when we left England ourselves.' Had that been
an accusation? If so, it had been very mildly expressed.

'I'd forgotten how beautiful he was,' she said. 'Just the
shape of his head, and that silky hair. Or *was* he beautiful,
though? Has he got better looking?'

She was speaking softly, half to herself. Alec seemed to
use this as a reason not to reply. He looked at Erin. He'd
come round to stand on the far side of the bed from Kate,
while Erin was still in the chair where she and Alec had each
kept their overnight vigil.

Erin found herself wondering, with a large dollop of name-
less suspicion, what had gone on between them at the airport
and in the car. If there was anything more to his hand on
Kate's back than comfort and support.

It horrified her to discover that she felt this jealousy and,
worse, that she couldn't read him. She hadn't known quite
how thoroughly he could retreat into the stiff-lipped reserve
that had been bred in him. She had seen it before, it was true,
but never this strongly, and she certainly hadn't seen it recently.

It was as if the Australian sun and—she dared to hope—

her own influence had softened him, made him open up like a flower in the daylight. Now he appeared to have closed off to her again. Closed to everyone, perhaps? And for how long?

'What do you want to do, Kate?' he asked her finally, his voice still croaky and tired.

She looked up with a sad, beautiful smile. 'Just to stay, I think,' she said. 'Could I stay here alone with him for a while?'

Once more, her gaze flicked to Erin. For a moment, an irritable frown pleated her brow, but then at last there was an acknowledgement.

'Erin! I'm sorry I didn't say hello,' she said kindly. 'Alec's been telling me how much you've done for William lately, and how much time you've spent at his side this week. I must thank you for that. It's...' She stopped and shook her head.

'That's fine. It was no trouble,' Erin heard herself answer, too brightly.

They were ludicrous words under the circumstances but, then, Kate's thanks had been incongruous and wrong as well. It was as if she was expressing gratitude for Erin nursing a sick puppy while Kate had been away on holidays.

But perhaps none of them knew how to behave in a situation like this. Did you follow your naked instincts? Or put a polite face on everything you felt?

In the background, Alec was answering Kate's question. 'Of course you can have some time alone with him. I've never tried to exclude you from his life, have I? And I never would.'

'No, you haven't,' she agreed. 'And I'm grateful for that, Alec.' She stood, leaned her thighs against the bed and reached across to squeeze his hand, then closed her slender fingers around his wrist. 'More grateful than I can ever say.'

Her voice was sweet and low and sincere, but Erin kept

remembering Mel's words of yesterday. 'If I want to see a one-woman show, I go to the theatre.'

If this *was* a performance, then it was an appropriate one. There were no jarring notes, no moments when the façade dropped. Erin found herself believing that Kate did care for William, and more than she had expected her to. It was right that this should be so. And on some level did William still remember her? His biological mother? Her scent and her voice and her touch?

If her presence here had any power to help the little boy, then Erin was thankful for it, but she was frightened, all the same, with a new source to her fears that hadn't existed this time yesterday. Angry, too, on Alec's behalf. He was the one who had put in most of the hard work with his child.

She thought, Perhaps I'm being selfish, again, too. I've wanted so much to build a relationship with William. I launched myself in without a backward glance and now, suddenly, no one will consider me any more. It'll be Kate's name on the hospital forms, Kate's feelings the nurses care about. Which is right. It *is*. But that doesn't mean it's easy for me. I should back off now, close up a little, protect myself a little before I get hurt. Before I come to hate her.

Over Kate's shoulder, she saw Alec's glance connect briefly with her own. He looked startled and ill at ease, and she realised how tense and hostile and suspicious she must look, fatigue etching each of these emotions more powerfully onto her face.

Once again, the frightening questions came to her. At the end of all this, when William was better again, what would Kate want? What would Alec want, and what would she herself be capable of?

She faced the next few weeks with dread.

CHAPTER SIX

THEY passed. The first two nightmare weeks passed.

For the whole of Mel's stay William remained on the ventilator, but the day before she flew home there was evidence that the paralysis had passed its peak and that he would be able to breathe on his own. Weaning from the machine would be gradual, with its cycle of artificial breaths slowly lessened in frequency and depth.

It would take several days before the tube could be safely removed, and even then William would remain on an oxygen mask for a further period of time.

Mel was teary when she left on a Monday morning. She had been a lifeline for Erin, putting aside any thought of a real holiday for herself and instead being available for both Erin and Alec whenever they needed her. She had even taken Kate shopping and relieved Rachel of her self-imposed burden as hostess several times.

It wasn't that Rachel disliked Kate. 'But when she's Alec's ex-wife, how am I ever going to love her, Erin? She's obviously been very well brought up. She's full of thanks and little gestures of gratitude. Tells me these lovely, confiding, gossipy stories about people I've been seeing on television for years. Hasn't put a foot wrong. But, still, I'm on *your* side!'

Erin wanted to tell her that 'sides' didn't enter into it, but held her tongue. Perhaps 'sides' would turn out to be crucial, as events unfolded.

She was teary about Mel's departure as well. They'd had some good talks, renewed their friendship. Mel was worried about Alec—about his new reserve, his careful politeness to everyone around him, his tight, strained face—and it had helped enormously to know that there was another person here who truly cared about him.

'I'll miss you. Come back and live in England?' Mel suggested to both of them, as she and Erin and Alec sat at the airport bar and had a last coffee before Mel's flight.

'Can't do that,' Erin said quickly and automatically, without thinking about it.

She hated any mention of the future at the moment, with its corollary reminder of the long road to full recovery that William still faced, of Kate's unpredictable desires and of Alec's and Erin's renegade wedding.

Alec still hadn't said a word about setting a new date, or anything about regretting the loss of their original plan, and Erin wasn't going to press the point. She knew what a strain it still was for him to simply get through the days. He was back at work, as she was, and they both spent as much time with William as they could. There were days at a stretch when Alec barely left the hospital.

Inevitably, though, Kate had begun to take a greater share in the vigil by her son's bed. Sometimes she read magazines or studied scripts as she sat, but mostly she simply stared at him, dozed at the foot of his bed or held his hand. Quite often, Alec was at her side.

There had been occasions, too, when Erin had come to visit William and had found Kate there asleep. She'd almost gasped at the classic beauty and poignancy of the picture the two of them made together—one so tiny and fragile and still, the other so vibrant and beautiful and Madonna-like.

Several celebrity-oriented magazines had got hold of the story of the actress's flight to her little boy's bedside, and there had been some articles about it, accompanied by a picture of Kate hurrying through Heathrow airport. The picture had been taken months ago, in another context entirely, but nobody mentioned that.

The fact that Kate's son had been in his father's full-time care half a world away hadn't been commented on either. In any case, Kate was a relatively new and minor star in the celestial landscape of the film world, so interest soon waned and the vigils she kept were private now.

'No?' Mel was saying, on the question of Erin and England. 'Not even for a visit?'

'Well, for a visit, of course,' Erin conceded. 'At—at some point. But, no, Mel, I can't plan. I— Don't ask me about anything, OK?' She spoke more aggressively than she'd meant to. 'I—I don't know what I want.'

It was an awkward moment. Alec was frowning at her, his face showing that same closed, patient, suffering yet unreadable look he'd worn since Kate had arrived. Or even before. The look that Mel was worried about. Mel apologised incoherently, though there was no reason why she should. She paused for breath, then launched at once, rather clumsily, onto a new tack.

'Hey, there's something I've been wanting to tell you both, but the moment hasn't been right, and now I'm running out of time. Could you handle some *good* news, do you think?'

'Sure, Mel,' Alec said dutifully.

His heart wasn't in it, Erin could see, despite the pretty blush on his sister's cheek, which suggested she'd really like it if she got a good reaction to this.

'Found myself a serious squeeze, I have. You're, uh, going to get a pretty horrible phone bill soon, I expect, Erin.'

'There's nothing to stop you paying her for it, is there, Melusine?' her brother growled.

'Yes, there is,' Erin cut in. 'I won't let her.'

'You will, as it happens, Erin,' Mel said. 'Because one of the things about him is that he's seriously rich. Only don't go accusing me of marrying for money, because I didn't even know that about him until I was in up to my chin.'

Erin reached across and squeezed her friend's hand. 'In up

to your chin, talking about marriage and you haven't said anything yet?' She gave a wobbly smile.

'Couldn't,' Mel answered. 'Kept wanting, well, a nice moment. It's been hard. Haven't been many of those! He's fabulous. You're going to love him.' She frowned at both of them, and added, 'When you eventually get to meet. He's gorgeous. Well, strangely no one else thinks so, not even his mother, but I do. And he rattles around in this huge stately home, which I love, only it's freezing, and he makes money out of about six different things, most of them to do with computers. He has a ponytail. He keeps goats. He designs things. And I'm sort of terrified he'll have forgotten me by now.'

'Despite the phone calls?' Alec suggested, trying hard.

'Despite everything.' She waved her hand. 'Sorry. Rattled on, but I just needed to tell you. Think of me. Know you don't have much time for that at the moment, but—'

'Shut up, Melusine,' her brother said, kind but weary. 'Of course we'll think of you.'

'Time to board?'

'Just about.'

So Mel left and Erin was alone in her little unit once more.

Not that she spent much time there. Today, she had an afternoon shift starting at three, and spent an hour with William immediately before that. Kate went and had her hair done, while Alec managed twenty minutes away from his work before an urgent summons to the gynae ward took him back to it again. He was on call tonight, and probably wouldn't leave the hospital again until tomorrow evening.

Kate returned to William at five minutes to three, smelling like a hair salon and apologising for it prettily. Erin kissed William, who was asleep, and went to deliver babies.

Two of them today. One was a first child who gave his mother quite a hard time. Her labour slowed after about fourteen hours and she was already pretty tired and discouraged.

Erin sent her and her husband off on a long walk around the unit, which didn't do anything. Alec appeared to examine another patient under Siobhan Dixon's care, and he and Erin talked to each other for a minute or two, although there wasn't really anything in particular to say.

Erin mentioned her patient's stalled progress, and when Tina McIntyre shuffled tiredly past again, holding her husband's arm, Alec said cheerfully, 'That's right. Wear out the floor.' Then he looked down at her thick socks and added, 'Actually, there's a corner of it that needs polishing, just here, I see. Want to slither over it a few times and give it a buff with your socks?'

Tina dredged up a laugh and immediately went into a contraction, the first in ten minutes. After this, they stepped up rapidly to every four minutes, then every two, and she delivered a healthy eight-pound girl, after an hour of strenuous pushing, at eight o'clock in the evening.

Alec was there. 'To catch the baby and take the credit,' Erin teased him, even though she knew he didn't attend deliveries in order to play God, but only to 'get my flying hours up', as he'd phrased it to her once. He summoned a thin smile for her humour.

Thin. Everything between them was thin at the moment. A thin quantity of time together. Gestures of affection thin on the ground. Thin smiles, thin laughs, so many thin places in the weave of Erin's future life that it was now nothing but holes. The only thing that wasn't thin was her desire and need for Alec, which remained as powerful a force inside her as ever.

When Erin's next patient, who was having an easy third baby, protested sweatily that she didn't want any more people present than she absolutely had to, Alec acquiesced and didn't come in, and Erin was torn apart by disappointment and relief.

By the time she finished her shift at eleven, Alec had been

called down to A and E, so she went up to the paediatric
intensive care unit alone, and entered it to find Kate still
there, and William... William...

William was *laughing!*

Oh, it was the best sound she had heard in weeks! Nothing
thin about it.

Erin stood back for a moment and simply watched. Neither
Kate nor William had seen her yet. Kate was absorbed in
entertaining him. She would hide her face behind a magazine
then peep out suddenly and exclaim, 'Peek-a-boo!' A few
simple variations on this theme—like popping out from the
opposite side of the magazine—were enough to keep the little
boy entertained for several minutes.

Erin had forgotten what a wonderful sound it was, this
darling little child's laughter. Such a rich, delighted gurgle,
so joyous and uncomplicated. And when she'd feared in her
darkest moments, over the past two and a half weeks, that
she might never hear it again, that even if William recovered
fully he would have been changed somehow by this illness,
made old and fearful and sombre before his time...

Oh!

She started to laugh, too, silently, with tears running down
her cheeks at the same time. Tonight William's laugh seemed
like so powerful and wonderful a sound that it could have
healed open wounds, built a bridge over a yawning chasm,
stopped two warring armies in their tracks.

She came forward, too happy to be conscious, as she usually was, of the uneasy relationship between herself and her
lover's ex-wife. 'Oh, Kate, just listen to him! You clever
thing! Hi, William! Hi, love!'

Impetuously, she hugged both of them, moving quickly
from Kate's rather stiff arms to William's still immobile
limbs. She blew a raspberry on his cheek and he laughed
again, and she felt as if she'd asked for the moon and someone had handed it to her, then and there, on a silver plate.

Kate immediately began to play it down, a tendency Erin had noted in her before and tried not to dislike. It had to be a pose, surely, that if everyone else loved a particular book, Kate hated it, and if everyone else considered something important, Kate couldn't even summon a yawn.

'It was just a little game,' she said. 'He does have a sweet laugh, though, I suppose, doesn't he? Don't you, angel? Yes, that's right, smile for Mummy.'

He did better than that. He laughed again, and then Alec appeared and he stopped laughing and said quite distinctly, 'Daddy!'

Alec shuddered and gave one single dry sob, then almost fell beside the bed. He didn't say anything, just knelt there holding William's hand. If Kate hadn't been there, Erin would have knelt beside him, holding him as hard as she could in her arms and pressing her mouth against his hair, because she knew he was close to completely breaking down.

But Kate *was* there, still sitting in her chair with a quiet smile of satisfaction on her face, and on the rare occasions over the past two and a half weeks when Erin had touched Alec in Kate's presence, she had sensed the temperature dropping. Kate definitely didn't like it, and Erin was *not* going to turn this into a territorial battle, as things stood.

Alec didn't need the tension. Neither did she.

And if it came to a battle, the doubts came seeping inexorably in. Who would win?

'I played peek-a-boo with him, Alec, that's all,' Kate was saying. 'I wasn't intending it to be a big moment.' She gave a shrug and a little laugh, then lifted her chin and smiled dreamily at both of them.

William's current night nurse, Wendy Keeler, came in. She was a skinny woman of about forty, with frizzy dark hair, a big freckle on her nose and twinkling blue eyes. Erin had met her a couple of times in the hospital cafeteria and had

found her conversation a little abrasive at times, but here in
the unit she was dedicated and cheerful.

'We're celebrating, Wendy,' Kate told her, still wearing
her languid smile. 'I played peek-a-boo with him and made
him laugh.'

'Terrific, Bill, you've got your sense of humour back!'
Wendy said.

'Please, don't call him Bill,' Kate put in quickly.

'Of course not,' Wendy agreed at once, 'If you don't like
it.'

'I hate it! Ugh!'

'It's my husband's name, actually.'

Kate was undeterred. 'I think it's the parents' prerogative
to decide which form of their child's name gets used.'

'Yes, you're right, of course,' Wendy agreed again. 'We
get so fond of them when they're here for a while, that's the
trouble. Start forgetting who they really belong to!'

'Well, don't, please!' Kate said sharply. 'It's bad enough
to think of him getting back to England with an Australian
accent…'

'Oh, he probably won't have time to pick up the accent,
will he?' Wendy said. 'You were saying earlier tonight that
you'd be taking him back within a week or two of his discharge, weren't you?'

'I haven't quite decided,' Kate said calmly, tossing her
head to flick her glossy hair back. 'There are some things to
work out first. I'm flying back to England in two weeks for
another film. I've been on the phone to my agent for nearly
three hours about it this evening! But I'll be back as soon as
that's over, and then I'll take him back with me. Alec, obviously we're going to need to talk,' she finished, in the same
matter-of-fact tone she'd probably used to her agent on the
phone.

Her liquid brown gaze met his abruptly raised face, steady
and wide-eyed. He was white, stiff, controlled. Hadn't an-

swered his ex-wife yet. To Erin it was obvious that he *couldn't*. Her own jaw was clenched painfully. She would have liked to have exploded. Into tears? Accusations? Some very, *very* plain talking to Kate?

All of the above, probably.

But with Wendy Keeler here... No, actually, it wasn't the presence of another person. She'd have held her tongue even if it had just been the four of them—herself, Alec, William and Kate. Because it wasn't her place to speak, to protest. She was the outsider in this situation. It was up to Alec to say...

'Yes, we need to talk,' he got out at last. 'In fact, in view of what you've just said, we're obviously overdue. I'm available whenever you're ready.'

Kate touched him. Betrayed a confidence and assuredness that Erin knew she could never have mustered under these circumstances. A light hand rested on his shoulder for a moment, then twisted gracefully to brush along his jaw, before pulling slowly—reluctantly?—back.

'You always said,' Kate reminded him softly, 'that whatever happened, I was still his mother. That you'd never close the door.'

'And I stand by that statement.'

'Well, you were right. You understood more than I did, back then. It's taken his illness to make me see it. I'm grateful, Alec. More than you'll ever know.'

'Yes. Are you?' he said, nodding.

Erin could see how hard he was struggling to maintain his façade of control, and his honour.

A lesser man might have ground out, Tough! You had your chance. You gave custody freely to me, and you can't go back on that. I'm the one who's given him the continuity of care. These days, odds are good that a court would see it my way, too.

But Alec would never behave that way. Kate knew it. Erin knew it, too, and wasn't surprised at his self-control.

In the background, William was singing quietly to himself, his voice musical with his sheer pleasure at being able to make sounds again. He had no idea that his entire future had just been tossed up into the air.

And what about mine? Erin thought. How much is Alec prepared to sacrifice? And will he consult me, or is it simply his decision?

'Erin, would you mind awfully giving me a lift back to Rachel's?' Kate asked her, moments later. 'Alec, you're going to stay, aren't you?'

'Yes.' He nodded tightly. 'Now's not the time to...' He didn't finish.

Kate yawned, then smiled and stretched, cat-like. 'I feel like something stuck to the bottom of a saucepan. Permanently!'

She rose, ready to leave. Erin hesitated. She desperately wanted to send Kate off in a taxi and stay here with Alec, but in the end she didn't trust herself. Could imagine, only too clearly, that she'd turn to him the moment Kate was safely shut in the lift to demand, Will you fight her on it?

But why? She was already certain that he would never deny William that relationship. He would go back to England, uproot his life again, rather than deny William the chance of being with his mother, and rather than lose William himself if Kate took him away.

Where did that leave her, then? Perhaps, at heart, that was what had given Alec his strongest motivation to come out here to Australia to claim her the way he had. He had needed a mother for William. But if Kate wanted her share of the child now...

What about me? she would demand of him. The question to which she did *not* have an answer. What does that mean about me? The words were already burning there on her tongue.

And since she was terrified that if she said any of this, they would fight and she'd say something unforgivable, or hear something unthinkingly cruel from him, she accepted Kate's hijacking of her services and they left the unit together.

In the car, after a short pause in the car park for a cigarette, Kate was absorbed in charting her own emotional growth over the past few weeks.

'You know, I think ·it's one of those dangerous myths we're fed as women—' she mused, then interrupted herself with a laugh. 'I'm a bit of a feminist, you'll have to excuse me! Anyway, I think it's a myth that maternal love automatically kicks in at the moment of birth.'

'Some people would claim it kicks in before that,' Erin murmured, but this was waved aside.

'I've discovered that that *epiphany*, I think I'd have to call it, can happen at as many different times and in as many different ways as there are different kinds of mothers. Of course, Alec will have told you about our doubts—over William, I mean. That he wasn't planned, and we weren't sure how to handle it at first. I think I was, well, swimming the Egyptian river…' She paused.

'In denial?' Erin supplied.

Kate laughed. 'You've·heard it before.'

'Yes. Sorry.'

'In denial, as you say, until well after Alec took William full time. I felt stifled. Not ready to think of myself in that new way. And things were so crazy for me with work, and so on. It's really only since I came here, and have had all those hours at his bedside.'

'Yes…'

'A chance to meditate, really. In fact, I think that's what William's illness, ghastly though it has been, has done for all of us. Given us a chance—a *second* chance, I suppose—to think about what we really want. And I know that what I want is for William to come back to England with me. It's so good to have that certainty at last!'

She didn't say anything further on the subject, didn't betray any apparent awareness as to how deeply her 'epiphany' would affect Erin's life. And perhaps she was right. Perhaps the fact that mother and son were going to be reunited was the only thing that counted.

The following weekend, Caitlin and Angus came down and stayed with Erin.

It was obvious to her at once that Caitlin must indeed be pregnant. She wasn't drinking tea, coffee or alcohol, and there were some sudden flights to the bathroom, where the taps would run noisily for several minutes. Angus would frown in that direction every thirty seconds, muttering something unconvincing about her 'not having shaken off that flu yet', and Caitlin would eventually emerge looking pale and sounding unnaturally cheery, as if nothing had happened at all.

Nothing was said about a pregnancy, however, and Erin respected Caitlin's and Angus's deep-seated anxiety on the subject and pretended that she hadn't noticed. Her heart ached for both of them, and she understood, on a more intuitive level than she would have understood even just a few months ago, exactly how hard this must be for them, after what they had already been through.

So perhaps Kate was right. Perhaps Erin had had an 'epiphany', too, following William's illness.

His condition continued to improve visibly with each passing day. He now had some movement in his upper arms, and had been given specially chosen toys to encourage him to use his arms and hands and strengthen the weakened muscles. He was eating normally by mouth again, but still seemed to have an acute sensitivity to certain tastes. He spat out most fruit juices as if they were poison, and approached each food he was offered with caution.

Erin and Alec had barely seen each other. He'd had some busy days at work, and he seemed to have retreated even more deeply into himself. Erin desperately wanted to ask him to talk, tell her what was going on inside himself, but as with Caitlin and Angus—only this was far harder—she forced herself to respect his apparent need for time and silence. Fought down, too, her longing to take him to her bed and somehow *brand* their love-making into his mind so that he'd never ever be able to do without it.

How could she demand answers about the future when he was hardly in a fit state to come up with them? How could she use their sensual response to each other to force the issue? How selfish would it be to come out with that cry of 'What about me?' that drummed in her head.

And it wasn't just her imagination—Kate was becoming more physical and more possessive with Alec. Every time they were together, she touched him in half a dozen different ways. More than once, she brought up memories. 'That time we went punting at Cambridge and you got stuck on your pole.' 'That three-day weekend we had in Rome.'

Was she aware that Erin knew this was when William had been conceived? Erin felt certain that she did…and guilty about her certainty.

Alec seemed to respond courteously to everything Kate said and did, as unreadable on this issue as he was in every other way at the moment. Did he want those soft-fingered clutches on his forearm? Those hips brushing past his shoulder as Kate passed his chair? The intimate use of 'we'? Or did he merely tolerate it all?

There had been no opportunity for intimacy between himself and Erin lately. She suspected he was too exhausted and too absorbed in William to even think of it. She felt almost guilty that her own need for him still burned so strongly, and though she sometimes hoped he'd simply drop in to her unit on his way home—she'd jerked awake more than once, thinking she'd heard a car pulling into the driveway and she dreamed of his body beside her, holding her, almost every night—he never did.

Rachel held another get-together that weekend, to celebrate Caitlin's and Angus's visit. The weather forecast wasn't good—clear skies but chilling down to an April frost—so it was an indoor evening, take-away pizza and ice cream for dessert. 'Embarrassingly simple,' Rachel said.

But it was the first remotely social occasion that Erin and Alec had been involved in since William's illness began, over three weeks ago, and she found that she had unreasonable hopes for the evening, despite the fact that Kate would be there.

These hopes were betrayed in the flowing skirt and figure-hugging top that Erin wore, in the make-up she used a little more heavily than usual, and in the fact that she chivvied Angus and Caitlin out of her unit and into Angus's sleek car and arrived with them at Rachel's a good fifteen minutes early.

'To help,' she said.

'What? Choose the pizza toppings?' Rachel queried.

'Tidy?' Erin suggested, looking at the litter of Archie's toys in the family room.

'To be honest, I'm not going to bother,' Rachel decreed. 'Peter and Lisa are coming, with their lot, and I've asked someone from play-group as well, with her family. If we pack it away, they'll only get it all out again.'

So Erin had little choice but to wait for another twenty minutes, rather on edge, until people began to arrive. Meanwhile, Caitlin and Angus went out 'to look at the garden'. A euphemism for Caitlin dry-retching behind a tree, as Rachel and Erin both knew.

'When do you think they'll tell us?' Rachel speculated covertly in the kitchen.

'When she gets to the second trimester,' Erin predicted.

'I expect so. I'll be crossing my fingers, even after that.'

'They will be, too, but I expect it'll be a relief for both of them when it's out in the open,' Erin said, speaking from the heart.

She ached for this same sort of relief herself—the relief of talking about the future with Alec, of seeing that mask of distance drop from his face and hearing about what he actually wanted. She didn't want to try and engineer such a talk, though, because every crease of tension she saw in his face told her that he didn't need that at the moment.

The play-group mother, Tanya, was the first to arrive with her family. Erin barely absorbed their names, and was happy when the kids gravitated at once to play, while Tanya's husband, Michael, accepted a beer from Gordon, and Tanya herself began to chat to Rachel. Peter and Lisa and their children arrived next, and last came Alec and Kate, entering the house like a couple, wrapped in conversation.

They had come straight from the hospital, and Rachel was eager for a report.

'He can hold a cup on his own,' Alec said. 'Very weak and wobbly, but he did it.'

'Still spitting out orange juice,' Kate came in. 'I'm worried about his vitamin intake.' She frowned and narrowed her eyes.

Tanya asked about him. What was the illness? How long before he would be out of hospital?

Her interest was all the cue Kate needed to take centre stage, and she came out with several statements that had Erin wincing inside, painfully conscious of the fact that Caitlin and Angus had returned from the garden and were both listening as well.

'Getting pregnant was one of *the* most effortless accomplishments of my life… Some women seem to inflate the whole childbirth experience out of all proportion, I have to say… I don't think you can really claim to know what parenthood's about—the pain and joy of it, all mixed together—for at least a year.'

Under cover of Kate holding forth, Erin asked Rachel, 'You haven't said anything about William at play-group?'

Rachel shrugged awkwardly. 'I haven't wanted to, Erin. I hadn't told anyone about you or Alec or William in the first place. The wedding, or anything. It all happened so fast. And lately… It's all become too complicated.'

So that after a while, as the noise level in the house rose, it became perfectly obvious that Tanya and her husband assumed that Alec and Kate were still married, and that Erin only fitted into the picture as Gordon's unattached sister. Conversation eventually shifted to other subjects, and the obvious moment for an explanation of the true situation was lost.

Kate could have said something if she'd wanted to, but apparently she didn't. Erin didn't want to pipe up with an assertion of her role in Alec's life. And Alec himself? He was wearing his habitual stiff, courteous mask.

Sickened, Erin realised that she didn't know, in any case, what to call herself any more. His fiancée? Six weeks ago, he'd bought her a beautiful wedding band in two colours of gold, inlaid with a sinuous string of tiny diamonds, but they'd skipped an engagement ring. When you had cancelled your wedding at thirty-six hours' notice, and hadn't scheduled another, were you still engaged?

Kate never looked as if she thought so.

Presumably, Alec still had the wedding ring somewhere at home, but he probably hadn't given it a thought.

The pizzas arrived and everyone ate. Erin was aware at every moment of exactly where Alec was in the room. When he laughed, she heard it, and when she saw that he wasn't eating much, her own appetite fled as well. The atmosphere became rather stuffy, redolent with the smell of cooked cheese, and Erin wasn't surprised to see Caitlin looking pale again.

As they cleared plates away into the kitchen, Erin suggested to her younger sister, 'Want to come for a walk?'

'Yes, please.'

But the fresh air came too late, and Caitlin lost her dinner in the gutter. 'This flu,' she managed.

'There seems to be a bad dose going around this year,' Erin answered her kindly.

Silence. 'You've guessed, haven't you?'

'Sorry, yes.' Erin didn't tell her that at least four other family members had as well. 'Want to just rest and breathe for a few minutes?' she suggested instead.

'Better, I think, yes. Not sure if my tummy's finished with me yet!'

They both sat down on someone's low stone front garden wall, hugging their jackets around them as it was dark and chilly now. The occasional car went past, and yellow light shone from people's windows. It was peaceful and pleasant, if a little tough on the rear end as the chill began to seep upwards from the hard stone.

'I've got to the ten-week mark,' Caitlin said, 'Which is a new personal record.' The humour was effortful.

'That's great, Caitlin!'

'And I'm feeling *so sick*! Which I know is good.'

'Good hormone levels. You'll go all the way this time.'

'Starting to hope so. Third time lucky, or something. I know a lot of couples go through a lot worse than this.'

'But that's no comfort.' Erin knew.

'You're not exactly having it easy yourself, at the moment, are you?'

'William's getting better. That's all that really matters.'

She was starting to sound the way Alec looked, masking her
inner feelings with polite platitudes.

'Is the wedding on again yet?'

'Don't know.'

'I mean, of course it's on, but—'

'It might not be on,' Erin said quietly.

'Has Alec said—?'

'Alec hasn't said anything. That's starting to tell its own
story, don't you think?'

'Give him time.'

'I am. I have been. Isn't easy. And I'm starting to wonder
if all I've done is give him time to decide that he and Kate
should have another try!'

'No! Oh, no!' Caitlin looked stricken. 'He doesn't look at
her that way.'

'Tell me honestly, though, Caitlin,' she muttered miser-
ably, 'does he look at *me* that way?'

'I— Well, I haven't seen— I mean, of course in—'

'Don't answer. I don't need you to. I can see it for myself.
He doesn't. Not any more. Mind if we head back?'

'Of course not.'

So they walked back along the cement footpath in silence
until, three houses away from Rachel's, Caitlin suddenly said
in a strangled, pain-sharpened voice, 'I'm bleeding. Oh, no!
Oh, what's happening? I'm bleeding!'

By the time they reached the house it had soaked through
her light-coloured trousers, and she went straight to Rachel's
linen cupboard, pulled out some towels to spread on the bed
in the master bedroom and lay down on it.

'Call Angus! Am I on these towels properly? I don't want
to muck up the quilt.'

'Caitlin, don't think about that!'

' My mother-in-law made it.' Her teeth were chattering. 'I
don't want to muck it up,' she repeated.

'I'll call Alec, too,' Erin said.

Angus paled at once when Erin told him, and hurried away in mid-sentence, from a conversation with Alec and Gordon. Alec followed, and Kate was hard on his heels, though no one particularly wanted her input.

'Bleeding?' she said in a carrying voice. 'A miscarriage, do you mean? Oh, it doesn't end, does it? It just doesn't end! What we have to go through!'

'We'll get you to hospital, sweetheart,' Angus was saying when Erin reached Rachel's room again. He was crouching by the bed, gripping her hand. 'Get an ultrasound scan done straight away, see what's happening in there. You've been feeling so ill. It's so different from last time when you had that slow bleed for days before the cramping when it ended. I can't believe this! I can't!'

'Is there any cramping this time?' Alec wanted to know. He stood at the far side of the bed, with Kate hovering behind his shoulder, her brows prettily knit.

'No, none at all,' Caitlin managed.

'That's good. Hold onto that, Caitlin. I can see that the bleeding is heavy, but that's not a conclusive sign.'

'I need the bathroom.'

'Tell me if there's any tissue, or if it's only blood.'

She nodded, got herself into Rachel's and Gordon's *en suite* bathroom and reappeared a few minutes later. 'Clots,' she said. 'As heavy as the miscarriage.'

'But no tissue? And still no pain?'

'Just blood.'

'Oh, God, Caitlin!' Kate breathed. She stood near the foot of the bed with her hands clasped over her heart, shaking her head slowly. 'After what I've been through these past few weeks with William, I want to tell you it's probably better this way. Half the time motherhood isn't something I'd wish on my worst enemy.' She gave a high, bitter little laugh. 'Be thankful for it, if you can.'

'Will someone just get her out of here? *Now*?' Angus muttered through clenched teeth.

Kate had heard, and she flushed. 'But I didn't mean...' She shook her head. 'I had no idea...'

'*Now!*' Angus repeated, even more harshly.

Standing near the head of the bed at Alec's side, aware of him as she always was, Erin felt as if the top of her head had just blown off after she'd spent weeks keeping her feelings in check by sheer force of will. She let fly in a low voice, the words tumbling out with not the slightest pause for thought. She turned to him, her eyes flashing as they connected with his.

'Could we at least spare my sister? Could we, Alec? Whatever I'm prepared to deal with from Kate—and I'm not sure how much longer I *can* deal with it—having Caitlin hurt like this is just too much!'

She was shaking with anger and built-up stress and didn't trouble to disguise the black look she flung at Kate. It contained all the dark, uncertain feelings she'd struggled not to feel about this beautiful, complicated woman for four years.

Alec turned and stepped towards his ex-wife. 'It's all right, Kate,' he said tightly. 'I expect you want to get back to the hospital.'

'No, I want to lie down. I'm totally shattered. Take me to your place, Alec.'

He ushered her out without another word, and Erin and Angus both let out the breaths they'd been holding and turned their attention to helping Caitlin out to the car. She lay down in the back seat with a towel pressed between her thighs, looking as if this was too shocking to cry about yet.

Angus took the wheel, jerked his car backwards out of the driveway, then drove off at a steadier pace into the night.

It was obvious to everyone that the party was over. Peter and Lisa took their children away from toys and playmates and bundled them into the car, parked in the street.

'Let us know, Rachel, won't you?' Lisa begged. 'I expect Angus will phone here first, won't he, when they know what's happening?'

Rachel nodded. 'Of course. I'll ring you straight away.'

'See you at play-group,' Tanya mouthed, her one-year-old on her hip, while Michael put the other two in the car. 'Thanks. I'm so sorry about Caitlin.'

Within ten minutes, the house was quiet.

'Want to hang out here, Erin?' Rachel offered.

'No... I should have thought to get a lift with Peter and Lisa,' she answered.

'Gordon will drop you home.'

'If he could, I'd appreciate it. Feel like some time alone.'

'I'll phone you, too, when Angus gives us the news.'

They hugged briefly, and Gordon got out his keys. Not one to waste words, he simply said as they drove, 'What is it they say? This, too, shall pass.' Then he finished cheerfully, 'Or, if you like, I could kill him.'

'Kill... Alec?'

'Time-honoured brotherly tradition in certain cultures.' He was a scientist by profession, and sometimes it showed.

'I'm not upset that you want to kill him,' she said bluntly. 'Hang on, no, that sounds—' She flung the mis-statement aside as too trivial to deal with. 'I'm upset,' she clarified, 'that you think I've got a *reason* to want to kill him!'

'You tell me,' Gordon invited. 'He's responsible for that Kate creature, hanging round like a blowfly in a sheep paddock. That'd be good enough for me. But if you want better reasons than that, you tell me. Got any?'

'Oh, Gordon!' She laughed. 'I'll keep you posted, OK? But, no, please, *don't* kill him!'

'No? Well, I guess that's a relief, really.'

For Erin, the relief lay quite simply in being alone.

CHAPTER SEVEN

ERIN'S solitude didn't last long.

Alec hammered at the door an hour later. 'Erin, are you there?' he called. 'I went back to Rachel's and she said—'

Erin opened the door. 'Come in,' she said quietly, her heart thudding.

'Can I?' He was slightly breathless, his chest rising and falling in a rapid rhythm.

'Of course,' she said.

'Kate and I have talked,' he began at once, prowling along her short hallway and into the kitchen.

Silently, Erin put on the kettle. Was this a legacy of growing up in a family of six children? she briefly wondered. Whenever there was a crisis, her automatic instinct was to bung on a cup of tea for all concerned.

Alec didn't look as if he'd be able to stay still long enough to drink it. With a stab of shock, she looked beyond the breathlessness, and noticed the tousled state of his dark hair, the fact that three buttons of his shirt were undone and that the garment was tucked crookedly into his jeans.

As if he'd dressed in a hurry.

'Talked?' she echoed, and there was a nuance of scepticism in her tone which he missed as he continued to bounce restlessly back and forth off her kitchen cupboards.

'She apologised,' he said quickly. 'That's…irrelevant, really.'

Erin frowned. Was it? It might be important to Caitlin!

She almost said something. Oh, Lord, a part of her longed so much to throw something, yell, issue demands, but he had plunged on.

137

'We talked about William and the future, and it's decided.' He stopped talking, prowled a little more. 'You probably know, don't you, that there's only one way this could go?'

At last he stood still, facing her, his eyes burning with blue fire. They were standing about two metres apart. On a bench behind Erin, the mugs she had got out sat next to the canister of tea. Behind Alec, the kettle began to bubble, shuddering against the bench-top on which it sat. It would click off automatically in about thirty seconds when it reached the boil.

'Yes. I think so,' she answered him. 'Kate will take William back to England, and you'll follow as soon as you can.'

It was hard to say the words. They came out wooden, and blunt-edged, around a big, hard lump in her throat. She folded her arms tightly across her chest, afraid that she'd have no control, that she'd suddenly launch herself across the cork-tiled floor and into his arms with the Kate-like cry of selfish need 'But what about *me*?' that hammered and burned inside her.

He nodded at what she'd said. There was a silence, then he spoke. 'This isn't what...I told you to expect a few weeks ago, with regard to Kate.'

'No,' she agreed.

'She had been so adamant that she was out of the picture.'

'It was William's illness,' Erin supplied. That lump wouldn't go away, and it sounded harsh. No wonder he read her words the wrong way.

'What? Should I not have phoned her that day to tell her?' he demanded.

'Of course you had to phone her!' Erin came in quickly. 'I'm not suggesting— I'm just saying, no one could have predicted his illness. It wasn't your fault.'

'She says now that it would have happened anyway, that she'd have come to realise, eventually, that she needed him in her life.'

Do you believe her? Erin didn't say it.

What had Alec seen in her face, though?

'I have to put William first, Erin,' he said quietly.

'I know that.'

'Which means making it possible for him to be with his mother on a regular basis.'

'Of course.' She nodded, too energetically. 'Alec, I *know* that. I understand it. Don't say it as if…as if I'm thick, or insensitive, or pathologically self-obsessed.'

'Hell, I'm not suggesting any of that!'

'What *are* you suggesting, then?'

'Nothing,' he answered. 'I'm presenting the facts. That's all. And I'm only happy that this all happened before the wedding.'

'Are you? Yes, you're right, of course.'

He gave a tiny nod. 'To give you…us…an easy—*easier*,' he corrected himself, 'way out.'

She struggled. 'You and Kate…will get married again.'

He looked appalled. 'No! What could have given you that idea?'

'Oh, your twisted shirt, maybe?' she suggested with dark sarcasm. 'Your mussy hair?'

He flushed with betraying colour. 'She tried—'

'Don't make excuses,' Erin snapped.

He looked as if she'd slapped him. His jaw jutted, his eyes glittered and his colour was still high. The tension in the air, the reluctant and intensely physical pull between them was like the crackle of electricity on the loose. Both of them fought it, and it seemed very separate today from the love they'd shared, a far more brittle feeling.

'I'm not, Erin,' he answered her, his voice oddly courteous. 'I wouldn't dream of making excuses for anything. Kate has come between us, hasn't she? I didn't think she'd be able to do that, didn't think it was even an issue, when she was in London and we were here, but William's illness changed a lot of things, and that was one of them. It gave Kate the power to come between us. Just how much do you hate her?' he appended in a conversational tone.

'Hate?' Erin bit out, shocked. 'That's a strong word. I don't hate her, Alec! She…has the prior claim, that's all. Over William. And over you.'

'She's not claiming me,' he insisted, then revised at once, 'Not the way she thinks she is.'

'Then how?'

Do I really want to know this? came the unvoiced question in her head, making her insides lurch sickly.

'Kate…' He sighed, then searched carefully for the right words. 'Likes to believe she is adored by all. That illusion was temporarily shattered tonight. She lost face. She was made to feel that she was insensitive. She's now set out to prove that that's not the case. I…' he sighed again '…have to limit the collateral damage.'

'You see her very clearly, don't you?'

'I didn't always,' he admitted. 'This is her survival strategy, that's all. We all have them. Perhaps she's not to blame for the fact that hers is rather all-consuming.'

'What's your s-survival strategy, Alec?' she asked, her voice cracking and going husky as it so often did at times of emotion.

Perhaps this was part of the problem between them. They simply didn't know each other well enough. The dramatic hurdles in their relationship had come too soon.

'My survival strategy?' He shrugged. 'Trying my best to do what's expected of me. To do what's needed in a given situation.'

'And in this situation?'

'We've covered that, haven't we? I'm going back to England once William is well enough to travel. Kate thinks she's coming back to get him herself, but on that, at least, she's wrong.'

But what about me?

'And—and me?' Just a thin, watered down version of the question.

'You've been terrific, Erin,' he reassured her politely. 'You've given so much time and care to William. So much support to me. None of this is your fault. Don't think that I blame you. In any way. In fact, I blame myself far more. I barged out here too quickly, bulldozed you with those wedding plans.'

'That's not fair either,' she said, her immediate instinct still to leap to his defence.

He laughed. 'Thanks, but I can take it, I think!'

'It was just…the way things worked out, Alec. The complications of modern life, I guess.'

'Is that the way we should look at it? All right,' he agreed.

He leaned back a little and his arm came into contact with the hot plastic side of the kettle. He frowned.

'Tea,' Erin said. 'I was going to make tea.'

But he shook his head, and she was relieved.

'I'll go,' he said. 'Even though William knows his nurses so well now, I still hate leaving him.'

And the fact that he thought she needed an explanation about this obvious fact underscored the emotional distance between them even more than hostile words would have done.

After he'd gone, she cried bleakly until interrupted by the phone, and since she knew it would be Angus or Rachel, with news of Caitlin, she went to answer it at once.

'Erin?' It was Angus, and she could tell at once from his voice that it was good news. 'The baby's still in there and doing fine,' he said. 'We saw it on the scanner, doing gymnastic routines like an Olympic athlete. The technician couldn't believe how active the little thing was. It was as if it wanted to let us know just how real it was, and we were both laughing, watching its little limbs moving about. It was great! Oh, I can't tell you!'

'That's, oh, Angus, that's fabulous!' she stammered. 'Are you coming home?'

'Yes, Caitlin's just getting dressed. The bleeding has tapered off to almost nothing now.'

'What do you think happened?'

'A tear in the placenta? Occasionally one twin will miscarry like that, but there's no evidence Caitlin was ever carrying two, so that seems less likely. She's going to take a couple of weeks off work, just in case, although that's probably an over-reaction on our part.'

And when they got back to Erin's unit twenty minutes later, they looked so happy that she hid her own feelings with a heroic effort, and rode out the time until they left after lunch the next day without them having guessed that her future with Alec was over.

Kate was due to leave at the end of the following week.

She had said something pretty and courteous to Rachel about 'not trespassing on your hospitality any longer', and had moved her three suitcases over to Alec's. Rachel was indignant and alarmed on Erin's behalf, and once again Erin took on the role of defending circumstances which privately had her far more upset than her sister-in-law could possibly be.

'It's not as if Alec is there very much,' she told Rachel.

'It doesn't take much. It takes amazingly little,' Rachel said darkly.

Erin gave up the pretence. 'It doesn't matter if something does happen,' she said. 'It's over between us anyhow.'

'Erin, no! How? *Why*?'

For several minutes she couldn't talk, could only sob wildly in Rachel's arms, her whole body jerking and shaking.

Finally she calmed down enough to make her thin explanation.

'Just turned out to be a fragile flower. Wilted under so much stress. Don't ask for a blow-by-blow account.'

'I will! Someday!' Rachel threatened frankly. She conceded, 'Not now. Just tell me how hurt you are.'

'Oh, how hurt do you think? Can't you tell? But it's not Alec's fault.'

Silence.

It goaded Erin to continue. 'Except insofar as he was the one with the baggage.'

'Ex-wife and child?'

'Exactly.'

'You sound bitter.'

'At myself, for ever believing it could be easy. These things aren't. I should have known…I *did* know…at the beginning. I let myself get swept away. I dropped.'

'*Dropped?*'

'Like a ripe plum. Into his open hand. Even though I'd yelled at him that I wasn't going to.'

'Shall I send Gordon round to put a brick through his front window and let down his tyres?'

'You two!' She summoned a half-hearted laugh. 'The violence! Gordon already threatened to kill him.'

'I know. I told him that was going a bit far, but I thought you might come at a brick.'

'You're joking, aren't you?'

'Of course I am, darling, but sometimes that helps, doesn't it?'

'The brick?'

'The joking, feeble though it is.'

'*You* help, Rachel,' Erin said. 'All of you. Gordon, Caitlin, Angus, Mel.'

Mel, whom Alec must have told.

Erin received a demanding e-mail from her, via Gordon's

computer, sadly lacking in punctuation and spell-checking. 'You never pikc up your phone, are you screening yoru calls or not at home, pls ring me!!!! What is this buisness of Alce and William coming back here wihtout you i dont udnerstadn.'

Erin didn't trust herself to ring Mel. Knew she'd cry, which was why she was, indeed, using her answering machine to screen her phone calls. Instead, she drafted a careful e-mail reply, which managed to avoid the confession that she didn't 'udnerstadn' either. Instead, it was full of the rationalisations that she gave to herself constantly, and to others when they asked.

That she and Alec had been too impetuous in the beginning. That the circumstances of them being torn apart and brought together again had been dramatic enough to suggest star-crossed love, whereas the truth, in the cold light of real life, was far more prosaic. What they'd felt for each other, expressed in all that white-hot physical longing and release, had not been able to withstand the onslaught of William's illness and Kate's re-entry into their lives.

It happened. Step-families were hard. The intrusion of an 'ex' was hard. Not all relationships managed to stay the distance. Best that it should have happened now, before the wedding.

Kate said the same thing, very kindly, to Erin the day before her departure. Erin was working an evening shift on the postnatal side of the unit, and took the opportunity offered by her dinner break to pop in and see William.

Her uncertainty on this issue was another nagging and relentless source of pain inside her. It was May now, two months since she had quite consciously decided to love Alec's son.

It hadn't been hard! It was as if there were a little switch in the middle of her back marked MATERNAL LOVE, and she had simply reached one arm over her shoulder and flicked it to the 'on' position. Unfortunately, she now discovered it wasn't nearly so easy to turn the damn thing off again!

She'd already lost Alec. Very soon she'd have to lose William, too. Of course she could simply have stopped coming to see him, severed that painfully tugging cord of new feeling with one clean, sharp slice, but that would have seemed like such a breach of faith to the precious, brown-eyed little boy.

So for his sake, and her own, she had determined on a gradual weaning away instead, the way babies with neonatal abstinence syndrome were weaned gradually from the drugs their mothers had taken during pregnancy.

She hadn't told Alec. Tried not to be with William when he was around. This, in fact, was why she was there now, on her dinner break. She knew he was doing an emergency Caesarean of twins and would be in Theatre for at least an hour.

She hadn't counted on Kate's presence, though.

William was no longer in a high-dependency unit, but had been stepped down to the general paediatric ward, where the atmosphere was considerably lighter. He had different nurses, and shared these new ones with other children, but his ability to communicate and move had increased markedly, so his ebbing illness was far less frightening for him and the continuity of care was less important.

When Erin peered around the door into his four-bed room at seven in the evening, she saw that Kate wasn't with him, and wondered if she should be ashamed of the relief that leapt inside her when she saw the unoccupied chair beside his cot. He was sitting up in it, propped with pillows, with a book opened on his lap, ignoring it as he watched two other, older children playing with cars.

'Ennin!' he exclaimed, catching sight of her and holding out his hands. 'Ennin! Truck!' He pointed at the other children. 'Brrm, brrm!'

'Yes, they're making the cars and trucks go brrm-brrm,' she agreed, while thinking, Who am I kidding with this gradual weaning away stuff? Maybe it hurts both of us more in the long run this way.

She asked the other children if they would mind lending William a few of the miniature vehicles, and the two of them spent several minutes playing with them on the cot blanket.

Then, suddenly, Kate appeared, holding a container of take-away steamed Asian noodles and vegetables. For a second, she froze at the sight of Erin, then recovered her poise and her instinct for the appropriate tone to take.

'Oh, it's so good of you to spend time with him like this, Erin!' she exclaimed sweetly, her tone subtly infused with surprise. 'Honestly, no one expects it.'

'I think William does,' Erin replied—gruffly, to her own ears. She wished, not for the first time, that she had Kate's light touch.

'He wouldn't notice. He gets plenty of attention. Too much, perhaps.'

'Do you think so?'

'I'd hate him to get spoiled by it, after all these weeks in here. I've told Alec that he mustn't pander to him.' She laughed. 'I've given him a list of dos and don'ts a mile long!'

'Have you?'

'It'll tide him over until I can get back here.'

'Do you know when that will be?'

'Two weeks. Three at the most. This new role is terrific, and fortunately the shooting schedule is very dense. Would you believe I have scenes with three Oscar nominees?' she drawled.

The indolent tone didn't fool Erin. 'That's fabulous, Kate,' she said.

She made it as sincere as she could, and didn't do a bad job of it. Her feelings towards Kate had no component of jealousy for her professional success, but it wasn't always easy to separate out the strands while your heart was still aching this hard.

Evidently, however, she'd done well enough for Kate to feel well disposed towards her.

She tilted her head to one side. 'This hasn't been easy for you, has it?' Her sympathy oozed like thick honey from a piece of honeycomb.

'No. Not very.'

Why is it that all I can mutter on occasions like this are these stout little agreements? Why can't I say something flamboyant and cutting and wonderful? I'm sure I *used* to be able to!

'But think of how much *worse* this would have been if it had happened after the wedding,' Kate pointed out gently. 'I know Alec already feels terrible—'

'Does he?'

'Yes, of course he does!' She spoke with a condescending authority that might well have been unconscious. 'About misleading you as to what he felt. About letting you down.'

'Are you and he...together again?'

Oh, bloody hell! Could we perhaps phrase it more delicately? Or not say it at all? That would be a better plan. More suspenseful, true, not to know what was really going on. But less naked.

Kate laughed. 'Depends who you ask,' she said.

'I'm asking you.'

'Yes, I've noticed! Well, no, we're not "together". I've told Alec that I don't think it would work. I'm not sure that he's...' She frowned. 'Well, no, he *will* accept it,' she decided firmly. 'He'll have to! I suppose from my perspective it would have been easier if you were married. But we can't always put ourselves first, can we?'

'No.'

End of conversation.

Erin couldn't stand it any longer. Not Kate's sweet insincerity, but her own replies, falling from her mouth like blocks of rough cement. Her dinner break was over, she hadn't eaten a thing, and she didn't even feel hungry, the savoury aroma of Kate's container of hot food when she opened the lid a moment later notwithstanding.

Erin went back to the postnatal ward, finished her shift without seeing Alec, slept badly and rang Caitlin in Sydney the next morning, only to come out then with all the clever, assertive, fluently spoken, double-edged lines she should have used to Kate the night before but hadn't been able to think of.

Caitlin didn't offer to commit any murders, lob any bricks or vandalise anyone's car tyres, but she *listened* as if she'd done a university degree in the art, and that helped. A little.

CHAPTER EIGHT

IF THERE had been both awkwardness and romance, rather deliciously blended together, in telling everyone at work two months ago that she and Alec were engaged, Erin found that it was simply painful to tell the same people that it had all been a mistake.

She knew Alec would tell those colleagues with whom he worked most closely—mainly other residents, registrars and senior obstetrics and gynaecology specialists. She had talked briefly with him about it by phone. But it was up to Erin herself to tell the nursing staff in the maternity unit.

She picked the afternoon shift hand-over on the Monday following Kate's departure and made a quiet announcement, offering a matter-of-fact version of the reason.

'Alec will be returning to England with William some time within the next six months. He and Kate have decided on an informal shared custody arrangement. There's going to be a lot of upheaval and a lot of people's needs to consider. And we discovered that what we felt for each other wasn't strong enough to overcome all that.'

There! An official version. And she had managed not to cry. If she had been Kate, she might have conspired with a publicist and made it into a press release. She didn't actually ask Siobhan, Tricia, Leigh and the others to spread the news, but knew they would do so—a couple of them casually, several of them kindly, one or two with a detour into various conjectures.

'Who do you think actually broke it off?'

'Does his ex-wife want him back?'

'I wonder what Erin isn't telling us?'

She didn't enjoy the thought of these questions, and when a couple more people actually asked them to her face, albeit tactfully worded, it was even worse. She had fallen in love with Alec without comments from the gallery, and she would have vastly preferred—needed, in fact—to tackle the task of getting over him in a similar climate of non-interference.

Looked like it wasn't going to happen.

Over the next few days, she was aware of people tiptoeing around her feelings in various ways. It was bitterly comical at times. Twice on Tuesday afternoon, Erin heard Tricia Gallant talking quite normally about a labouring patient until she realised that she was about to say Alec's name in Erin's hearing, at which point she suddenly dropped into what was almost a stage whisper to finish her story.

On Wednesday evening, Siobhan tripped over one of the ball-shaped metal wheels at the corner of the file trolley, purely because she was so eager to beat Erin to the birth suite's kitchen to make tea. Alec had just walked in there himself, hard on the heels of Erin suggesting a 'cuppa' to her colleagues at the nurses' station, and, yes, on seeing him she had hesitated for a tell-tale few seconds before getting to her feet, drowning in familiar feelings, and kind Siobhan had leapt into the breach.

'No, I'll make it, Erin...'

Crash!

'Yee-ee-ouch!'

Thud! Siobhan sat heavily in the nearest chair, clutching her foot and grimacing. Erin felt as if the incident had been entirely her own fault.

'How about *I* make it?' offered Kelly Norman, a midwife in training, and Erin went back to filling in her patient's details with hot cheeks, even hotter ears and an aching gut as a chatty conversation between Alec and Kelly floated out of the kitchen and along the corridor.

I've been here before, she realised. Back to Hans Christian

Andersen and *The Little Mermaid.* I'm walking on knives again, the way I did two and a half years ago.

Only this was far worse.

Back then, in London, she'd only imagined—painfully and guiltily, because he'd been engaged to Kate—how it would feel to hold his hard, hot body in her arms, wake up beside him with their limbs still tangled together, look into his blue eyes across a table set for two and talk about shared plans. Now she knew. She'd tasted the sweetness of his love, like drinking fine wine. Doing without him was like drinking brackish, tepid pond water instead.

'Here's your tea, Erin,' Kelly said.

'Thanks.' She looked up with a smile as she took the mug, then saw Alec over Kelly's shoulder.

'You were right about Cathy Cloder, Siobhan,' he said. 'No sign of cervical ripening at all, and she's at day fourteen overdue. I'll be surprised if the prostaglandin gel does the trick. I went through her history again, and she seems sure of her dates.'

'No sign of trouble with her non-stress test,' Siobhan offered in reply.

'Still, it always makes me nervous. Post-term babies can have problems. I expect Dr Blake will want me to start a drip first thing in the morning if we don't get some action overnight. Erin, who have you got?'

He tacked the question onto the end of his comment about the other patient. It took her by surprise, although it shouldn't have done. Like any committed resident who hoped to become an obstetrician himself, Alec was interested in being on hand for as many deliveries as possible, particularly anything out of the ordinary.

And he wasn't the sort of man who would behave differently towards her just because of their difficult personal circumstances. In fact, he would bend over backwards not to let it make a difference.

She struggled hard to do the same.

'Primi,' she said, using a common shortening of the medical term for first-time mother. 'Thirty-two years old, thirty-eight weeks two days' gestation. No problems during the pregnancy. Came in at the appropriate time with her husband and seems cheerful and in control so far.'

'Did you do an internal?'

'She wasn't keen so, no.'

The current policy at Black Mountain Hospital was to leave well enough alone in that area if the patient was happy. Internal examinations to check the extent of cervical dilation were uncomfortable, and many women didn't like them. Others wanted an idea of how far they had come, and how far they still had to go, measured in centimetres from one to ten.

'No problems, then?' Alec said.

Which was, unconsciously, exactly the impression Erin had wanted to give, she realised.

Get out of my delivery room, Alec! This one's going to be easy and I don't need or want you!

Was that behaving normally? No!

He got called down to A and E shortly after that, to help treat a heavily pregnant patient with an asthma attack, so Erin finished her tea in peace and went back to her patient.

It was quiet this evening so far. Just after seven. Still plenty of time for things to hot up before she went off at eleven, but at this stage she, Siobhan and Tricia each had only one patient, with Kelly floating where needed. The other two labouring mums were likely to deliver before Erin's first-timer. In fact, she'd probably be handing Donna Moss over to the night staff, still as pregnant as ever, when she went off at eleven. An external manual exam revealed that the baby was still high, suggesting that Donna had a long way to go.

Another hour of slow progress confirmed this probability.

'I think I will have that internal,' Donna decided at half past eight. 'Maybe even an epidural, too, if I've got a long way still to go.'

She was starting to sound discouraged, having already laboured at home since that morning before the contractions had stepped up to a frequency which had warranted coming in. She held her bespectacled husband's hand tight while Erin put on gloves and felt the cervix.

'Nice and thin,' she reported, 'but only about three centimetres dilated, I'm afraid. You can have an epidural if you like. Plenty of time to think about it.'

'Maybe not quite yet, then,' Donna decided. 'I'll see how I go.'

'Shall we go for another walk?' John Moss suggested, and his wife nodded.

'Can you please help me up, love?'

At this point, the whole thing suddenly went from being slow and routine and almost tedious to being anything but. Donna's waters broke, splashing half on the bed and half on the floor.

'Something's coming! The baby's coming!' she yelped in a panicky tone a few seconds later.

But it wasn't the baby, it was a loop of cord. It squeezed forth as soon as she lay back on the bed, and Erin had to think on her feet, lightning fast.

'This isn't good, is it?' Donna was saying.

'No, I'm afraid not.' She pressed the emergency button as she spoke. 'Can you get up on your hands and knees, Donna? The knee-chest position? Hips high, head low.'

A contraction came, paralysing Donna with its intensity, and she reached for her husband, moaning.

'It's all right. It's all right,' he kept saying, but he'd turned green with fear.

Tricia entered the room and reported that Alec and a senior obstetrician were on their way as well.

'Try and work through the contraction, Donna,' Erin coaxed. 'We need you up in this position.'

And what they didn't need was the baby's head, pressing down on the cord and cutting off the blood supply. It would be fatal to the baby if the cord was compromised for long. It had looped further out, and Erin had no choice but to push it back manually, to keep it safely moist in the vagina, while Donna remained in the knee-chest position. Tricia began to apply external pressure on the baby itself, pushing it back up as high as she could against Donna's ribs and lungs.

'What's going to happen?' John demanded hoarsely.

'We're doing fine here, John,' Tricia reassured him automatically.

Another contraction came. They were stepping up now that the waters had broken, so that Tricia and Erin were working against nature in forcing the baby higher.

'I can't breathe. This feels awful!' Donna gasped. John was running his hand down her back, his lips dry and white.

'I know,' Erin said, 'but we have no choice, Donna. We have to keep the baby's head from pressing on that cord.'

'We're going to start getting you ready for Theatre,' Tricia said. 'You're going to have a Caesar, love. We need to get that baby out quickly now.'

'Will it be OK?' John asked.

'Yes, because Donna was in here when it happened,' Tricia assured him, patting him on the back. 'We have theatres up and running round the clock here, and we've taken action quickly.'

'Just stay in that position, Donna,' Erin came in.

Alec arrived with obstetrician Perry O'Hare hard on his heels. The senior doctor immediately confirmed what Erin and Tricia had already known. An emergency Caesarean was the only safe way out for this particular baby.

There was a flurry of activity as they took Donna downstairs. Alec would assist, while Dr O'Hare handled the inci-

sion and the delivery. There would be a paediatrician waiting
for them in Theatre, but Erin would receive the baby into her
care if it was healthy.

Poor father-to-be John had to wait in the unit as the urgency of a cord prolapse required the more rapidly acting
general anaesthesia. Husbands were only permitted in
Theatre when epidural anaesthesia was used. As they entered
the lift, Erin could hear Siobhan saying to him sympatheti-
cally, 'Can I get you a cup of tea?'

Donna had a difficult journey to Theatre. She was still on
her knees with her head down, terribly uncomfortable and
shaking with effort and tension. Her breathing was shallow,
with the pressure of the baby on her lungs.

Tricia had stayed in the unit so Alec was the one now
forcing the baby higher, and he managed to keep his hands
placed correctly as they moved. It had to be working, because
the cord was no longer being forced out, and Erin didn't need
to use her own hand to keep it within the vagina. When
they'd checked the foetal heart rate before starting the journey down to Theatre, it had still been strong.

Staying close to Donna to reassure her, Erin kept bumping
against Alec's shoulder. He trod on her toe. They each apologised—she for the bump, he for the toe—then gave up because it just kept happening. And anyway, was it really
crushed toes and jarred shoulders they were apologising for?
Of course not...

Donna began to heave and gag, and there was the sound
of liquid splashing onto the floor. They ignored it and hurried
on. Someone else would clean it up.

Theatre. Bright lights. Staff waiting. Operating table lowered at one end so that gravity would still assist in keeping
the baby high in the uterus. Anaesthetist Jeff Adler began his
work at once, inserting a drip and taping it in place, checking
his monitors, calculating the dose.

Erin stood back while others scrubbed and prepared. Her

job was the baby now. Paediatrician Anna Parker asked her quietly, 'What happened? She was already in the unit?'

'Yes, and I was in the room. When her waters broke, she said she felt the baby coming, and I knew she had to be wrong because two minutes earlier she'd only been at three centimetres after labouring all day.'

'So that cord wasn't compromised for long?'

'Hopefully not at all. We were all pretty quick and she was great, kept her head down, let us push that baby around through the contractions.'

'Good. I hope I'm not needed, then.'

Dr O'Hare was ready to make the incision. Standing beside him, Alec looked as if he would have liked to do it, but Perry O'Hare wasn't going to let a junior colleague loose on this one. He talked through what he was doing in a controlled mutter, his hand working with an efficiency and speed that Alec could not yet have fully matched, although one day he would be every bit as practised as this.

Erin saw how he watched every movement, his eyes lowered so that all she could see were his lids and lashes. As always, her heart lurched and her love and longing for him became something physical, actual and aching inside her. It wasn't easy, having to work with him in an emotional environment like this.

'Here it comes. A boy,' Dr O'Hare said, pulling the baby out.

The first time she'd seen a Caesar, Erin had been quite shocked at how quick and rough it was, just a wet, slippery heave with firm hands, over in a second. She was used to the sudden drama of it now, used to the blood and to the sweet moment when the baby cried—this one with a strength that told them all he'd do fine. There was a surge of relief and pleasure in everyone, expressed in talk or smiles or exclamations.

'Beautiful!' said Perry O'Hare.

'Thank God!' whispered Helen Tarlington, one of the theatre nurses.

Alec gave a brief, bright grin of satisfaction, which faded at once to sober concentration as Perry O'Hare handed the rest of the job over to him—the careful drawing out of the long, pale cord, the delivery and examination of the placenta, the slow process of stitching the uterus and closing the incision, while Jeff Adler did his balancing act with the anaesthesia.

Erin helped Anna Parker with the baby.

His Apgar score was seven at one minute and nine at five minutes, he weighed in at a perfectly respectable 2950 grams—around six and a half pounds—and she was able to transport him back up to the maternity unit while Alec was still at work over Donna's incision.

He didn't look up at her as she left, although she glanced across at him more than once, hope like a sharp-edged stone in her chest.

I've got to stop doing this, she realised as she took the newborn baby up in the lift. I can't keep waiting for *moments* between us. They're not going to happen. And if they do, they'll only be painful.

He's so good at soldiering on. If he'd been the Rostrevor son who was supposed to go into the army, instead of Simon, I can imagine he'd still be there, facing his future with the same tight, focused expression that I see on him sometimes now. He still cares about me. I'm sure he does. As a friend, perhaps. Or even something more than that. A girlfriend whom he still wishes well. But it's not enough. He didn't care for me *enough*.

Not enough to want to add her as a permanent ingredient to the complex mix of his life. More emotional baggage. A second wife, with the inconvenient habit of demanding occasionally, 'What about me?' When, of course, he had to put William first, and Kate a close second, while what those two each needed from the other jostled for priority of place as well.

In all that, something had to give, and it turned out to be what he had with me.

She hadn't expected or wanted to see him again that night, but it happened anyway. She took the newborn boy to see his father, who was still waiting with a mug of unwanted, half-drunk and now tepid tea in the birth suite.

John Moss turned as he heard her enter the sitting room where a television burbled away in the background, and his face looked panic-stricken, then glowing.

'This is…?'

'Your healthy son,' Erin said happily. 'He's perfect, John. We got him out before there was any significant damage to the cord.'

'Does Donna know?'

'Not yet. She's still under general anaesthesia. She'll be in Recovery soon, and you can go down to her, but I expect she'll want to hear that you've held him.'

'Oh, *can* I?'

'Of course.'

She gently scooped up the tiny, swaddled form and put him in his father's arms. He looked like a pomegranate in a pale knitted hat, and he had a jazzy little set of silky black sideburns like a miniature Elvis, and hardly any nose at all. He was so precious and new and alive, however, and plain faced, dumpily built John was so overcome with happiness and relief that the moment had the beauty and poignancy and warmth of a classical oil painting.

In no hurry to have it end, Erin was happy to answer all John's questions—about Donna's well-being, about the Caesarean delivery, about what to expect over the next few days. They took the baby along the corridor to the postnatal ward and got his Perspex cot set up in a two-bed room that was currently empty, although a sign saying MOSS/O'HARE was already slotted into place at the end of the bed.

'Does he have a name?' Erin asked, when everything was almost settled and John had asked several more questions.

John looked blank. 'Er, we decided on something on the way into hospital,' he recollected vaguely. 'But I've forgotten which one it was.' He thought a little harder, and came up with, 'That's right! Either Benjamin or Christopher.'

When Alec came into view a few minutes later, however, his first hearty words clouded the issue somewhat. 'How's Richard James, then, John?'

'Richard—? Was *that* what we decided?' He frowned and looked doubtful.

'According to your wife, yes, but admittedly she was only a few minutes out of anaesthesia.'

'No.' He shook his head. 'I'm *sure* it wasn't Richard.'

'Would you like to go down and see her and get it sorted out?'

'Yes, please!'

He left at once, and Alec and Erin were alone in the room with Baby Boy Moss. A few weeks ago they would have laughed together over the confusion about the baby's name, but today Alec simply frowned and muttered something that was impossible to understand.

He strode out moments later with a hand pressed to the back of his head, suggesting a headache. The angular movement of his body betrayed the degree of strain and discomfort he felt in her presence now.

She gave a jerky sigh and schooled her face as midwife Kathy Waller entered to check up on her new charge.

'Who's this little man?' she asked.

'There's some confusion about that,' Erin answered, her tone overly bright. 'So for now he's just Baby Moss.'

A few minutes later she was back in the birth suite. She tidied up Donna's delivery room, preparing it for its next occupant, then went to finish up a couple of administrative jobs at the desk. It was almost ten now, and she looked forward to going off duty.

Then she heard Alec's voice coming from Room Three, and only then realised that he was back here as well. Her heart lurched, then sank. Would they manage to avoid each other? Doubtful.

The place was noisy at the moment. There were two mums in loud, active labour, getting close to delivery, and a third who'd come in an hour ago. Obstetrician Larry Cotterill came barrelling through the swing door that led to the private patients' suite, yelling, 'Where's that resus. trolley I asked for?' Kelly went hurrying off to get it.

'This is a junkie mum, I hate to say,' Tricia reported to Erin, coming out of Room Three.

Erin remembered the last baby with an addicted mother that she'd helped Alec to deliver a couple of months ago. The tiny, premature girl that had died.

'I'm going to give her to you for your last hour, lucky you,' Tricia said wryly.

'I can handle it.' She squared her jaw and fought down her instinctive reluctance.

'And I'm going to get another doctor up here as well, because I think my lass in Room One will need a Caesar,' Tricia added.

She grabbed the phone and Erin went into Room Three, narrowly missing a collision with Alec—his familiar scent, his hard chest—in the doorway. They clutched each other's arms, let go at once, apologised jerkily and sidled through the door.

'Damn, damn, damn,' Erin said under her breath. She encountered other obstetrics residents and registrars in the unit just as often as she encountered Alec, but the encounters with him were, of course, always the painful ones.

'Sorry,' he muttered uncomfortably over his shoulder. 'I'll

be back when there's more happening.' He stopped where he stood, and elaborated, 'I got a pretty honest history, I think. Partner was co-operative.'

Erin was pleased to see that this mother-to-be had her partner, Paul, with her. He looked ill at ease, but was focused on Marla Driscoll's well-being. He had a cup of ice chips in one hand and a warm wheat-pack in the other, and he was urging her to try a shower.

'OK,' the thin young woman agreed, and Paul helped her out of her clothing and into the steaming needles of water which Erin turned on in the adjoining private bathroom.

Marla had visible track marks on her arms, bad skin, bleary eyes and uncared-for teeth, but she obviously loved her partner and was concerned for his well-being. 'Sorry I'm dragging on you…' Erin heard. 'Don't have to stand here getting all wet, darl!'

The shower didn't last long. 'I need to push!' Marla said, and Alec couldn't have been far away because he appeared again in seconds.

The two of them helped Marla to find a comfortable position, which turned out to be standing beside the raised bed, leaning her head and forearms on it as she bore down. Alec coached her with his usual calm and quiet warmth. She pushed effectively, and it took just three contractions, with barely a pause for breath in between, to bring the small baby out.

'A girl? Wow!' Marla said, then crawled onto the bed and lay still.

'You did so *great*, Marla!' Paul was saying. 'She's beautiful! Heaps of hair!'

But already, within a few minutes of birth, the baby began shaking with narcotic withdrawal, her cry jagged and distressed. Erin laid her on Marla's stomach, hoping the warm body contact would help.

Marla grimaced and again said, 'Wow! She can cry, can't she? That means she's strong and healthy, I guess.'

But then, without warning, the baby fitted. It was a frightening sight, tiny limbs jerking and head thrown back. Alec abandoned his delivery of the cord and placenta and strode out to the medication room. He was back quickly with a syringe and a dose of phenobarbitone that brought the fit to an end within a remarkably short time.

With the baby swaddled and back in her arms a few minutes later, Marla was in tears. 'What happened?'

Alec took a deep breath. Watching his face, Erin knew he would be warring against his instinct to be angry. You couldn't afford that, because the goal was to get addicted mothers to feel comfortable enough to seek treatment and keep in contact, and they were often so easily scared away by guilt or fear.

'Marla, you have a baby with severe narcotic withdrawal,' he said gently. 'We're going to deal with it so that she suffers as little as possible. She'll be taken to our paediatric intensive care unit, where she can receive morphine on a carefully reduced schedule until she's lost her dependency, and ultimately she'll be healthy and happy.'

'How long will that take?'

'It varies with every baby. We'll keep an eye on her, and help you do the best for her that you can.'

'I decided I'd stop using when it was born,' she said rather defensively. 'I'm going to go on the methadone programme.'

'That sounds like a good decision.'

'Someone—some counsellor—told me I could still breast-feed.'

'On methadone, yes. On heroin, no.'

'Didn't realise they were that different.'

'I told you they were,' Paul came in. He had been soothing her and the baby at intervals in a low voice.

'Paul doesn't use any more,' Marla explained. She offered

the information as a positive development in her own life, which, of course, it was. 'Stopped before we met, di'ncha, Paul? Keeps telling me to go to support groups and stuff. I told him one thing at a time, OK? After it's born?'

She was starting to shake, but whether it was an emotional response or a physical one Erin couldn't tell.

It was eleven o'clock already. Permanent night shift mid-wife Emily Anderson arrived to take over while Alec was examining the intact placenta. Erin brought Emily quickly up to speed on the patient, her partner and her baby, scribbled some notes out at the desk and then left the unit.

It wasn't easy to leave a patient at this point after delivery, but it would be a good hour or more before Marla and her baby were settled, one in the postnatal side of the unit and the other up on PICU, where William had spent all those difficult days.

William.

Erin still went to see him at the start and end of every shift. During breaks as well, when she could manage it. If Alec was already there, she tiptoed out again, but tonight she knew he was still dealing with Marla and the baby.

William was asleep, of course. Perhaps it didn't make sense to be doing this, but somehow she just couldn't let it go. Like Marla Driscoll with her heroin dependency.

Was it as destructive as that? Hardly! But she no longer knew who she was doing it for. William? Herself? Alec, per-haps, because she knew he wasn't able to be here as much as he wanted to be, and that it distressed him.

William lay under his white sheet and light, open-weave blanket. He looked tiny and still in the cot, but was blessedly on the way to recovery. He was having regular physio-therapy, and it had started to seem very hopeful that he would be one of the seventy-five per cent of children who recovered fully from this rare, frightening illness.

I won't be with him to see it, Erin thought for the hundredth time. If Kate comes to take him home, I won't see him running and climbing again.

That hurt.

Alec had said, in the heat of the moment, that he wouldn't let Kate take William home until they were both ready, of course, but whether he'd hold to that, Erin didn't know. He might change his mind. He might have done so already. She was no longer privy to his decision-making and his plans.

Sitting in the chair by William's cot, she made a deliberate effort to let go for a while, to enjoy the sight of his peaceful, normal sleep without letting her own needs and troubles cloud the picture. The sound of his breathing wafted to her ears, heavy and rhythmic, almost hypnotic. She felt the tension draining from her limbs, heard the intermittent, familiar sounds of the ward as soothing ones, and dozed off before she'd realised there was a danger of doing so.

She didn't know how long she'd slept when she felt a hand gently nudging her shoulder. *Did* know, before she even dragged her eyes open, that it was Alec. Her body always recognised him somehow.

'What are you doing here?' he whispered.

She blinked and covered a yawn with her fist. 'Spending the night, apparently,' she joked, aware of his warmth and scent and the brief imprint of his hand even though he'd withdrawn it at once. 'Sorry, I didn't mean to fall asleep.'

'But why did you visit him?' He was frowning. 'There wasn't a problem, was there? I didn't get any message.'

'No, no problem. Nothing like that,' she answered him quickly, then watched as he pulled up another chair and sat, holding onto one bar of the cot as if it were William's hand. 'I...always come to kiss him goodnight.'

Alec looked shocked. 'I didn't know that.'

'Why should it be such a surprise?' she asked defensively. 'Did you think I was just manufacturing what I felt for him when he was ill and in those weeks before that?'

'No, of course not,' he responded automatically.

It was the kind of polite, expected reaction he might have given, on an empty stomach, if someone had asked him, 'Mind if I take that last sandwich?' At some level, he *did* think exactly that, Erin realised. That her care had been purely tied to a sense of duty about her future role as William's stepmother. And his next words confirmed the fact.

'I just thought,' he clarified carefully, 'that you might have been happy to let it slide a little sooner. I'm glad you didn't.'

'Why?' she demanded, surprising herself with the aggression in her tone. Why was she pushing this?

'Because it means something that you still care for him.'

'Don't make me feel like this, Alec,' she gasped. 'I don't want to!'

The legs of the chair scraped on the vinyl tiled floor as she stood up abruptly and went to the window, staring out into the night to hide her tears. In her blurred vision, she could see traffic lights on a near-deserted road on the far side of an expanse of eucalyptus trees changing from green to red.

Seconds later, she felt his shoulders and chest fitting across her back, and his arms cradling her from behind. He didn't say anything, just held her. He must have been able to feel the way her sobs were shaking her, though, and she wished that he *would* speak. Didn't care what he said, just needed to hear *something* in the cool, familiar voice that she loved. Something that would bring a safe, acceptable end to this.

She heard his breathing, felt the warmth of it against her hair and neck, and longed to swing around and bury her face in his shirt, but managed to hold back. Every nerve ending already clamoured for him, sang at his touch. The thought of betraying any more of her need to him—*for* him—appalled her.

He made a little sound of pain and frustration in his throat, and she could feel his muscles tightening. He was fighting something. His physical need for her? It could only be that. Just as she was fighting it so hard herself.

Her body had come to *expect* certain things in regard to Alec Rostrevor—the touch of his mouth on hers, his hands on her skin, the warm, soft scent of him in her nostrils, a mix of clean cloth and soap and skin. Her body didn't know it wasn't supposed to feel like this any more, that it wasn't supposed to go on *wanting* and exulting in him like this.

'What can I say?' he whispered tightly at last. 'What am I allowed to say in this situation? Nothing!'

'No, nothing,' she agreed quickly. 'Nothing, Alec, OK? Don't make it any worse than it has to be.'

'I had a phone call from Kate a couple of days ago,' he said in a new tone, his arms still around her.

'Yes?'

'They've got a new version of the script or something. She's not going to be finished shooting her scenes as soon as she'd hoped.'

'Is that good?' Give me some rules, Alec. Tell me what to feel.

'William wouldn't have been ready to go back with her if she'd been able to get out here when she wanted to. He's still not close to walking, or even crawling, and that's just the physical part. In that sense it's good.'

'Mmm.'

She could feel the vibration of his voice against her back, intimate and distracting with its reminder of how they'd lain together in bed like this, talking lazily in the night.

'On the other hand, she'd begun to establish her relationship with William again, and now the disruption to that is going to be longer. When she was out here, I was hoping she'd say no to the film, that she'd consider the cost of it in other areas, but—'

'You never asked her to? To say no to the film?'

He stiffened and let her go at last.

'I don't beg,' he said, his tone hard and firm. 'If she couldn't see for herself—or if she didn't consider, herself, that such a sacrifice was warranted—I wasn't going to blackmail her into it.'

'Lord, Alec, I never mentioned blackmail, did I?' It came out more angrily than she had intended.

'Even on a subtle level,' he argued, drawing back even further. 'People have to make their own decisions. Like I had to, when I threw away my career in finance years ago. Or, God, like that drug-dependent mother tonight,' he went on quickly, as if his own past wasn't something he wanted to go over again. 'A part of you wants to grab them by the shoulder and say, Stop using! Look at what you're doing! But it's their decision, and if anyone else tries to make it for them, it won't work. Any pressure will have the opposite effect. If I think I'm going to have to apply pressure, I back right off.'

'Are we still talking about Marla Driscoll?' she asked.

His face was clouded, frowning, and she could tell that his mind was crowding with memories and emotions.

'Yes,' he nodded, focusing on her again. 'But about Kate, too.' He paused, then added scratchily, 'About you, too, for that matter, Erin.'

'Me? What pressure have you applied to me?'

'None. That's the whole point, isn't it? That's what I've just said.' His blue eyes met hers steadily. 'I don't, and I won't. I did at first, when I came out here, and that was wrong of me. I bulldozed you into those wedding plans. I apologise for that.'

'No, Alec, I—'

'All right,' he agreed. 'That's water under the bridge, isn't it? But it's up to you how much time you spend with William now. It's up to you how you prioritise your life.'

She frowned. What was he holding back?

Something.

There was a subtle downturn to the shape of his mouth, a tightness around his eyes and two hard little balls of muscle near the hinges of his jaw, which her fingers itched to caress away. That he meant what he said, she didn't doubt. But she knew that it cost him to say it, and that inside him there was some sort of rebellion going on.

They stumbled through an ending to the conversation, and she made her escape as far as the lift. Waiting for it to arrive, she leant her palm on the cool metal panel beside the doors and tried to work it out.

What was he battling? Their starting and their finishing point had been William and her continued visits to him, so she felt it could only be that. Despite what he'd said, and what he clearly thought he ought to feel, did his heart tell him she shouldn't go on claiming a connection to his son?

Accepting this in small, unwilling steps as she drove home, Erin knew that she faced a severing of the last real emotional link between herself and Alec. She could almost hear the violent sound of it as the chain in her heart stretched and twisted and snapped.

CHAPTER NINE

FOR a week, Erin and Alec saw little of each other.

Erin's roster had changed, and she would now spend one day each week in the antenatal clinic, keeping her skills fresh in this area. Generally, it was very pleasant work. Most of the mums were happy about their pregnancies and keen to find out how they were progressing. Sometimes there were grumbles about symptoms, and sometimes there were danger signs which necessitated tests or a referral to the doctor.

There were one or two problem patients as well—women who weren't looking after themselves as they needed to, and women with background issues that required intervention and support.

The rest of her working days were spent on the postnatal side of the unit, where Alec's appearances, like those of the other doctors, were more regular and predictable. He came in the mornings to give postpartum check-ups to newly delivered mothers, and he checked babies prior to discharge.

Erin fell into the immediate habit of scanning the patient list at the nurses' station for danger spots. Shorthand notations such as 'LUSCS', which stood for Lower Uterine Segmented Caesarean Section, or 'PROM 36/2', meaning Premature Rupture of Membrane at thirty-six weeks and two day's gestation, signalled the greater likelihood of his presence in that patient's room.

But she could often avoid him on this side of the unit in a way that she couldn't in the birth suite, with its atmosphere of greater urgency. Here, her main role with most of the mothers was education—how to take care of a stitched tear, how to bathe a newborn and look after its cord stump, how to breast- or bottle-feed, and how to change a nappy.

If she paused in the doorway and saw him busy with her patient or another midwife's, she could usually murmur a plausible, 'Oh, sorry. I'll come back when Dr Rostrevor is finished.' If he was aware of her, he'd give a token nod and a perfunctory smile. Sometimes he didn't even look up, and she thought he probably hadn't heard.

On a Friday morning at just after nine, exactly two weeks after Kate's departure, Erin summoned her reserves of…well, was it courage? Control? Probably both. She sought Alec out during a quiet moment to give him back his key. She'd taken all her things back from his place and had no need to go there any more.

It ought to have been an easier task than returning an engagement ring—the one he'd never had time to give her—but somehow it wasn't. A key was actually more intimate than a ring, she found.

A ring spoke of the future. It was the token of a promise. Something longed for but not yet real. A key was about everything that had already happened, all those precious times with him which she had now lost. It was about the right to come and go as convenient, to make free with his space, to share it and claim it as equally her own.

"Um, could I see you for a minute, Alec, in the flower room?' she asked him.

She had stood up at the nurses' station and succeeded getting his attention. Now she crossed to him quickly as he left the two-bed patient room that was just across the open area in front of the nurses' station's high, curved front desk.

'The flower room?' He looked blank, disconcerted.

'It's…more private there,' she explained awkwardly.

In fact, though, there was someone there—a new grandmother, deftly arranging a large bunch of pink and cream flowers in one of the odd assortment of vases that had accumulated over the years when patients left them behind. She smiled at them, however, having finished her task.

'There!' she exclaimed in satisfaction, and carried her pretty burden out carefully.

Erin had the key already in her hand, a small piece of shaped metal, warmed by her body heat.

'I need to give you this,' she said to him clumsily, and held it out between her thumb and forefinger.

'Oh. Right.'

He recognised it at once, nodded and reached out for it. Their fingers touched briefly, and she wondered how such a tiny moment of contact could mean so much to her, stabbing her with a deep, inner desire. He didn't reattach the key to his keyring, just dropped it into his pocket as if he didn't want to waste any more time on it. Perhaps it simply wasn't important to him.

The moment was over. Erin's heart was still hammering painfully, and she felt sick, wondering what she'd expected to happen. A scene of some kind? She needn't have hauled him away from his work like this. Should have simply put the thing in an envelope and left it on the desk at the nurses' station for him to pick up at his convenience. Now they were standing here, he with his back to the open door and she facing it, not knowing what to say next.

'I did find…uh…a sock of yours that had fallen down behind the laundry basket,' he said. Socks! They were reduced to trafficking in socks! 'It had parrots on it. Crimson rosellas, I think.'

'Oh, right. Those.' She nodded, though she hadn't yet noticed that one had been missing. 'Just put it in my—'

She broke off, and he turned, following the direction of her open-mouthed gaze.

That wasn't Kate. That couldn't have been Kate, walking briskly along the corridor. She'd been visible, in the view offered by the open doorway, for less than a second, and it had to be a tribute to Erin's state of mind these days that she had apparently started seeing Alec's ex-wife in any slender, copper-haired visitor that walked into the unit.

'Pigeon-hole,' she finished in a vague tone.

'Is something wrong?'

'No. It's fine. It's nothing.' She shook her head vigorously.

'Thanks for the key, then.'

'I thought you might need it back.'

'I'll get the sock to you in the next few days.'

'There's no hurry.'

'It's washed.'

'Thanks,' she said pointlessly, then…flash!

There again, through the open doorway, heading back along the corridor in the opposite direction. Two more graceful strides. Slim legs clad in figure-hugging black trousers. A bounce of bright hair. An air of self-satisfaction, importance and urgency. Beauty spilling around her like golden flame, leaving sparkles in its wake.

This time, Erin was sure.

'Kate!' she called abruptly. 'Kate, come back! He's here!'

'*What?*' Alec wheeled around.

Erin pushed past him. 'I saw Kate,' she said. 'I'm sure it was Kate. Looking for you.'

'She's supposed to be filming in Scotland.'

'Well, she isn't. She's here.'

'Alec?' came Kate's voice as they both turned into the corridor, Erin ahead and Alec close in her wake.

'Kate!' He came past, his shoulder brushing carelessly past Erin's as he stroke forward to meet his ex-wife. 'What on earth are you doing here?'

She took both his hands in hers, then stood back and laughed. 'Your face, darling! I knew you wouldn't believe it! Since they changed the shooting schedule, I managed to wangle a week off and I came by taxi straight from the airport. I've come to take William home, Alec.' Her voice fogged.

'Home?' he echoed blankly.

'And I'm hoping you'll be able to come, too. Or at least to follow within a few weeks.'

'No!'

'Are you that indispensable to Australia's pregnant mums?' she teased lightly.

'I'm talking about William, Kate!' he said impatiently. 'He's not ready for a trip like that, halfway around the world, and with a woman he hardly knows.'

'Oh!' She gave a stricken little cry, took a step backwards and pressed her palm to her cheek as if he'd slapped her. 'My God,' she whispered. 'I didn't deserve that, did I? I know I haven't been the best—'

'It's not a question of what you deserve, damn it. It's not *about* you at all!' he said, his teeth clenched. 'It's about William, and I'm simply stating facts.'

'I thought you were behind this, Alec. I thought you wanted it. Me being his mother.'

Her voice was cooler now, and she was angry. The fog of emotion was gone from her tone. Erin was rooted to the spot, with an absurd desire to protect them from the curious ears of passers-by. She wanted to shepherd them both into the flower room and shut the door, but she couldn't yet find the strength to move.

'I do,' Alec said. 'That *is* what I want. But not on your terms, Kate!'

'I think you're wrong! I think he is ready!' She rounded on Erin. 'This is because of you, isn't it, you silly, trivial little Australian? You won't let him go.'

Alec cut in before Erin could reply. 'This has nothing to do with Erin. Hell, I wish it did!'

His eyes flicked to her and she was caught in his gaze like a terrified animal.

'Why, Alec—? But it's *you* who—' Erin fumbled.

Kate didn't wait for her to get the words out. 'Can we leave Erin out of this, Alec? In your e-mail a few days ago, you said he was almost crawling.' She had regained her confidence already. 'And I suspect the plane flight will be a lot easier with a child who's not mobile yet!'

'I'm not talking about the flight. I'm talking about continuity of care, and emotional needs, and—'

'Please,' Erin interrupted desperately at last. 'Give yourselves some privacy!'

Alec turned to her, blank-faced. 'I'm sorry, I—'

'Don't apologise. I'm thinking of—'

'Yes. Yes,' he agreed impatiently. 'You're right. Come on, Kate…'

He took her by the elbow and pulled her into the flower room. The door closed behind him, and Erin was left alone in the corridor. Alone, that was, apart from two straggling morning visitors who looked at her burning cheeks and glittering eyes curiously for a moment before becoming absorbed once more in their own concerns.

Shaking, she went back to the nurses' station and groped about in her mind for what she should actually be doing. Sandy Owen had wanted a lesson in bathing her baby. Annette Carpenter was exhausted after a long, painful delivery and a baby who'd kept her up all night.

Erin had put a 'Mother is sleeping' sign on her door and had taken the baby away to the nursery for an hour or two. Now she could hear that he was awake and fussing, probably in need of a feed. She wheeled him in to Mrs Carpenter, then went to the adjoining room to bathe little Alicia Owen.

And every time someone walked into the unit for the rest of the shift, she would look up, hoping and half expecting to see Alec, her heart already pounding in her ears, her throat already tight.

He didn't appear, and she didn't go and visit William in

the paediatric ward on her way home at three. Simply couldn't stand the possibility of seeing Kate.

At home, thinking unenthusiastically about dinner at twenty past six, she was still trying to school herself to the idea that it might be days before she found out the result of Alec's tense exchange with his ex-wife when there was an impatient hammering on her door, and she knew it would be him.

'Did she win?'

The question spilled out before she thought, while he was still standing on her doorstep. The clear evening air was already chilly, and he wore a lightweight, semi-waterproof jacket in dark grey over his conservative hospital clothing.

'Win?' he echoed. 'No, of course she didn't win! Can I come in?'

No! Have to deal with his effect on her in the confinement of her little town house? No, thanks!

'No, if you want to talk, I'd rather grab a jacket and come out.'

'Go for a walk?'

'Yes.'

I think I'd start screaming if I had to stay in the house.

She didn't say it, but he could probably read the words in her face.

'Fine.' He looked just as pent-up. More so, perhaps.

She took her forest green leather jacket out of the hall cupboard and shrugged her way into it, checked the pocket of her jeans for keys and closed the door. They began to walk briskly but aimlessly along the street, in silence for a good minute until he suddenly repeated, 'Of course she didn't win, Erin!'

He was walking a little ahead of her, as if too emotionally charged to match her slower pace. His hands were balled into fists in the front pocket of his jacket, and if he hadn't been almost yelling, she'd have thought he was talking to himself, not to her.

'I know she's had a lot of influence in all our lives just lately,' he went on. 'But where William is concerned, I'm not going to move. He's not ready to travel, and I can get his doctor's opinion to prove it! I've agreed on four months, and David Kamm confirmed it.'

'Why are you here?' she demanded. 'I thought perhaps she'd brought up some crisis. You look—'

'I'm here because I've snapped,' he cut in. 'I've royally snapped my twig, Erin.'

He stopped abruptly and wheeled across into her path, his arms out like a trap…into which she immediately fell. It happened in a second. One moment she was striding along with the chilly evening air against her face, the next moment she was cradled in his arms in the darkness, beneath a large gum tree on the nature strip beside the street, imprisoned by an urgent, imperious hold.

She was slammed at once with a wave of awareness. The breath left her lungs and she gasped for more air, already on the point of tears. The fact that he was trying to kiss her didn't help. The fact that she wanted so badly to let him do it was worse. His head was bent. His mouth briefly seared across her cheek, and he groaned.

Hating her weakness where he was concerned, she fought him off before it was too late, balling her fists and pressing the backs of her hands into his stomach, wriggling like a child in a tight sleeping bag.

'Erin!' he said desperately.

'Oh, no, Alec Rostrevor!' she retorted, still backing away. 'I am not here for you when it's convenient, or when you need me, or when there's no one else.' She half stumbled off the kerb and into the quiet street. 'Don't you have Kate for that?'

'No! Kate?' He took a step backward now, as if horrified. 'As in a lover?'

'Yes. She wants it, doesn't she?'

'No, she doesn't! Haven't I said that? She wants the power of promising it, she wants to keep me dangling on a string. She needs to believe that she was the one who ended our marriage, and that if she said the word I'd come running back to her. But she won't say the word because she doesn't really want me.'

'Is that really how it is?'

He spread his hands.

'Yes! She knows in her heart that we don't have the capacity to make each other happy. It pleases her, though, to tug on that string she's convinced I'm attached to every now and then. That's *all* that goes on between Kate and me in that sense, Erin, so can we at least dispose of that issue as a barrier between us?'

'OK,' she conceded. 'All right.' She flung out her arms extravagantly. 'Disposed of.'

'That's not all, though, is it?'

'You're saying that as if the fact that we—as if our break-up was my fault.'

'Fault? Do we have to deal in faults?'

'You mean because it always takes two?'

'True, isn't it?'

She pivoted and began to walk away, unconsciously imitating his earlier pose of hunched shoulders and hands in jacket pockets. 'In this case,' she flung back at him, 'I think it took four.'

'You, me, William and Kate,' he agreed. 'Plus a hemisphere. Isn't that the crucial thing?'

'A hemisphere?'

'That's what I wanted to say tonight. When I said that I'd snapped.' He took a deep, jerky breath. 'This is no good, Erin. I can't do without you, and I came to tell you that. I

know what I'm asking of you—to love not only me, but
William as well. And to tolerate Kate. And I realise that
perhaps asking you to live half a world away from your family and your home on top of all that, is too much. You said
so, the day Mel left. And I thought then, Well, that's it, isn't
it? Because I knew by then that Kate wasn't going to take
him staying out here. But I can't— God, the thought of losing
you... I said I wouldn't beg. But here I am, doing it. Could
you *please*...love me...enough to put up with Kate...and
make your life in England...with me?'

His face was white and his lips looked tight and numb.
He'd hardly been able to bring himself to say the words.

'Y-you m-mean...you *do* love me?' she stammered. 'You
do want me?'

'Has that ever been in doubt?' His face still smoked with
pain.

'Yes, oh, yes, Alec, it has!' she answered him. 'I
thought— When we had that talk the day Caitlin thought she
was losing her baby and we decided it was over, I thought
it was coming from you. That *you* felt there was too much
baggage, too many conflicting needs. You never asked me to
come to England with you!'

'You'd said to Mel that you wouldn't. Said it straight out.'

'In the heat of the moment, because I was too scared to
think about anything to do with the future. I hadn't known
then that Kate would want to take William back with her.'

'And you told me that you couldn't tolerate Kate any
longer. Kate will be in England, a part of our lives, and—'

'Don't take so much notice of what I *say*, damn you!' Erin
was half laughing, half crying, and shaking from head to foot,
all of which evidently warranted his arms around her, stroking her back, and his lips pressing against her hair. She bur-
rowed her forehead into his shoulder, her strength vanishing
into thin air. Oh, she needed this! 'Only take notice of what
I feel, Alec, *please*!'

'And what's that?' he whispered. 'Let's get it straight once and for all, shall we?'

'I love you, and I love William, and I'd tolerate Kate if she were a set of identical triplets living in the flat upstairs, for the sake of having the two of you in my life. I've faced her now. I know her, and I can take it. Of course I'll come to England!'

'Don't say it like that,' he urged. 'I'm asking you to give up your home.'

'You were willing to give up yours when you came out here.'

'It didn't matter. Compared to living without you, it just wasn't important. *You* are my home, Erin.'

'I feel that way, too, and if I'd known you thought— Why did we both think the wrong things about each other so easily?'

'Because of the baggage,' he answered simply. 'Because of all that was happening. And because of the mistakes I made at the beginning.'

'What mistakes?'

'Not trusting how quickly and deeply you could care for my son. Rushing you into the wedding. Not letting you do it the way you wanted to.'

'You were right, though. It's the marriage, not the ceremony, that's important.'

'Get a little selfish, would you?' he urged, only half joking. 'I saw those bridal magazines on your coffee-table.'

Alec ran his finger along her jaw and down her throat, stopping only when her jacket got in the way.

'You did?' The words melted into his soft, teasing kiss.

'The night I stayed there with Mel,' he said against her mouth. 'Just before Kate arrived. We're going to take our time over it this time around, with a honeymoon for three at the end of it when William is well.'

'Mmm. I'd…like that,' she admitted.

'See? Helps to tell me what you really want.'

'Hey, isn't that the sound of a very well-used pot calling this kettle black? When there's so much *you* didn't say?'

'True,' he conceded, then fell silent, obviously thinking hard.

Erin did the same, nestling more deeply into his arms. What was it he'd said just last week, the night in William's hospital room after they'd delivered Marla Driscoll's drug-dependent baby? 'I don't beg.'

She hadn't fully understood the words at the time. Still didn't, perhaps.

'Why don't you beg, Alec?' she asked him.

'I'm sorry?'

'You told me last week that you don't beg, that you don't apply emotional pressure. That was *me* you were talking about. And the question of going to England. I didn't understand. I still don't. Why is it so hard?'

'I kept thinking that you would have told me if you were willing to go. Till now, I've spent my life always knowing exactly what other people wanted. Wanted for themselves, and wanted of me.'

'I would have told you if I'd known...been able to believe...that you loved me that much.'

He sighed. 'We both seem to have a hard time with talking about what we want. You, I've discovered, because you care about the people in your life.'

'And in your case because your parents never treated that as worthy of consideration.' Erin suddenly understood. 'This is a pattern for you, isn't it? That you go along, bound in iron bands of duty, with what other people expect...'

'Until I crack,' he agreed cheerfully. 'Have to tell you, this is the best and nicest crack-up I've had in a while.'

'Best, nicest and *last*, I hope.'

'Should be. I've got a higher percentage of the things I want out of life at thirty-one than many people ever achieve, and I'm going to hold onto them. If you promise me that living in England isn't a sacrifice for you...'

'Don't you remember what you said a few minutes ago?' she reminded him softly. '*You* are my home.'

'Oh, Erin...' He kissed her until the sweetness of their mouths was mingled together.

'This is what I want,' Erin whispered. 'To love you like this, wherever we need to be, and whoever needs to be a part of our lives.'

'Then will you marry me?' he said.

'When I think about it,' said Caitlin Ferguson, 'it was very nice of you to still have me as your matron of honour, Erin, when I looked like the back end of a bus.'

'Back end of a bus? No, you didn't!' Angus said as he came in, looking over her shoulder at the album of wedding photos she was leafing through with Erin.

The three of them were standing in the drawing room of the large, comfortably modernised two-hundred-year-old cottage in Kent which Erin and Alec had bought the previous year. The place had views of the village church, horse paddocks over the back fence and a big, old-fashioned garden which clamoured for attention and then rewarded it handsomely.

'Thank you, darling,' Caitlin answered her husband fervently.

'No,' Angus went on, considering the matter. 'You were only six months then. More like the back end of a van. It wasn't until you reached the eight-month mark that you got to be the size of a bus.'

'Ah. Right. That's what you meant,' Caitlin drawled, then said again, with a major revision of tone, 'Thank you, darling.'

Her warm reception of Angus's arms sliding around her

waist suggested she was comfortable with his humour, however.

'Gorgeous album,' she told Erin. 'I've only seen the ones
that Gordon took, and they weren't exactly professional.'

Erin leafed through the pictures of the church wedding
down near their parents' place on the coast, followed by those
of the reception at a cliff-top restaurant with panoramic views
of the ocean. Then Caitlin paused for a moment, listened and
said, 'Uh-oh, there goes Emma.'

She hurried upstairs to collect her eighteen-month-old
daughter before Emma's cries woke the other sleeping baby
in the house. Erin's son, Thomas, was just two months old,
and not sleeping very well yet, by day or by night. Erin had
soothed him off in his bassinet half an hour ago without a
feed, according to some expert advice from a book, and had
threatened to burst into tears herself if anyone or anything
woke him before, at the earliest, half past three.

Kate Gilchrist, unfortunately, hadn't been around to hear
this dark announcement. While Caitlin was upstairs and Erin
was still leafing through the wedding album with a tired smile
on her face—Angus had lost interest by this point, and had
gone in search of Alec and William, who were planting an
ambitious array of vegetables in the ancient kitchen garden
Alec had finished unearthing from a blanket of ivy and weeds
a few weeks ago—Kate's pert, noisy little sports car roared
around the herringbone brick semi-circle of the driveway and
screeched to a sudden halt. The sound of the handbrake being
wrenched on squawked in the clear spring air.

She sprang out of her car before Erin could put away the
album and reach the front door. Then she pelted up the steps
in a pair of impractical pink mules, rang the doorbell loudly
and called 'Hall-oo, you lot!' in a ringing tone, for good
measure.

On cue, there came a wail from the nursery, and Erin
sighed.

'Come in, Kate,' she said, hiding her irritation as she opened the door. 'Thomas has just woken up, if you'll excuse me, but William is in the garden with Alec.'

'Sorry I'm late.'

'He hasn't noticed yet.'

'I'll have to borrow your booster seat for him.'

'Alec will get it out for you.'

'You're a saint, aren't you?' Kate said lightly.

Erin just laughed as she went up to Thomas. She'd heard this backhanded accusation from Kate before. It obviously pleased Alec's ex-wife to believe that she was a painful thorn in Erin's side, but actually she wasn't. They saw her too infrequently for that these days, a fact which bore out Alec's wisdom in never pressing for a formalised arrangement of shared custody.

When Kate knew that she could have William whenever she wanted him, she tended to put off her visits, and the little boy, now over three years old and fully recovered from his illness, was secure enough in Alec's and Erin's love and happy enough in his daily routine to greet his biological mother—Erin was the one he called 'Mummy'—like an unexpected present.

Much appreciated, thanks, but not vital to his well-being.

'Kate's here,' he would say excitedly, and go off for an afternoon of expensive spoiling, usually involving ice cream, fast food and new toys.

He would come home tired and grumpy, and could be a little difficult for the next couple of days, but it only happened approximately once every three months, now that Kate's initial enthusiasm had waned, so it wasn't a serious problem. To him, Kate was like an extra and oddly youthful grandmother.

Speaking of grandmothers…

Alec's parents were coming to dinner that night to meet the visiting Australian relatives. In this context, it was Alec who accused Erin of sainthood, but again it was an appellation she felt she didn't deserve.

A happy marriage was like an emotional fortress, she had found over the past twenty-one months. Protected by its warm, strong walls, she could look out at other people's foibles with equanimity.

Whenever Mrs Rostrevor let forth one of her carefully manufactured little digs about Alec's poor life choices, he and Erin would simply let their gazes catch and hold for a second, a blend of amusement and heat, and let it go.

'How did you score that one?' he might mutter to her a few minutes later.

'Oh, only a seven out of ten. Points for originality, but it wasn't very well worded, was it?'

Mel had accidentally overheard their scoring system a few months ago, so they had to be careful about it now, because she'd collapse into gales of giggles if she knew they were doing it.

Mel had married her titled, wealthy and un-handsome lover last June in an eccentric ceremony featuring a small boat, waterlilies, peacocks and a pond, and they were now intent on producing an heir. As long threatened, Mel had given up nursing and was working on a novel.

'Thickly disguised autobiography,' she claimed. 'Only not about me.'

The fact that she was now Lady Mel and had a husband with millions of pounds in the bank meant that nothing was said by the Rostrevors to warrant a scoring system of her own.

'Life's not fair, Alec, is it?' Erin said to her husband, when he appeared in their room with freshly washed hands and mud on the knees of his faded jeans.

He took small, crying Thomas out of her arms.

'I heard him from outside,' he said. 'Are you going crazy?'

'No, I'm absolutely happy, actually,' she said, meaning it

'Ah. You've already gone crazy, then. No sleep for two months, and you're happy.'

'Blissfully.'

'So am I...' He kissed her softly on the mouth. 'Listen, lie down with him, forget what the book says, give him a feed and drift off to sleep, both of you. It's obviously what he prefers, and why shouldn't he? Drifting off to sleep in your arms is certainly one of his father's favourite activities. Kate's heading off with William for the afternoon. Angus is taking Emma for a walk. Your sister and I will cook a rack of lamb and chocolate mousse for my finicky parents.'

'You see,' Erin answered. 'That's why I'm blissfully happy. Because I've got a husband who knows what I want, without even having to ask.'

'Wasn't very hard this time,' he said softly, holding Thomas in one arm and pulling Erin close against him with the other. 'You want sleep.'

'Mmm, sleep,' she agreed.

'We worked out all the difficult wants two years ago, didn't we? Now all we're left with is—'

'Sleep,' she repeated with longing, and yawned.

'Go to bed, then, darling.'

He pulled back the cool, soft duvet, pushed her gently down onto the bed and nestled Thomas into the crook of her arm. She kicked her sandals to the floor, pivoted until she was horizontal, sighed and yawned once more. Then Alec covered her up, gave her a final sweet, lingering kiss, touched his lips to Thomas's plump cheek for good measure, let himself out of the room and quietly closed the door.

Modern Romance™
...seduction and
passion guaranteed

Tender Romance™
...love affairs that
last a lifetime

Sensual Romance™
...sassy, sexy and
seductive

Blaze
...sultry days and
steamy nights

Medical Romance™
...medical drama on
the pulse

Historical Romance™
...rich, vivid and
passionate

29 new titles every month.

*With all kinds of Romance for
every kind of mood...*

MILLS & BOON®

Makes any time special™

MAT4

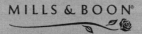

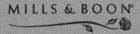

MILLS & BOON®

Medical Romance™

A CHRISTMAS TO REMEMBER *by Margaret Barker*

Part 3 of Highdale Practice series

Dr Nicky Devlin sees Jason Carmichael's desire for her as the perfect chance to repay him for the pain that he has caused her friend. In the run-up to Christmas she realises she loves Jason and the accusations against him turn out to be lies. How can she convince him that her feelings are real after all?

THE DOCTOR'S DILEMMA *by Lucy Clark*

Part 3 of The McElroys trilogy

Falling in love is definitely not on the agenda for ambitious bachelor Dr Joel McElroy. But living and working with the warm-hearted Kirsten Doyle reveals to Joel that she needs some TLC herself. With the arrival of Kirsten's orphaned niece, Joel finds himself drawing closer to this ready-made family—and facing a dilemma…

THE BABY ISSUE *by Jennifer Taylor*

Part 2 of A Cheshire Practice series

Practice Nurse Anna Clemence has tried to keep her pregnancy from gorgeous Dr Ben Cole, but in his desire to get closer to her, he discovers a closely guarded secret. Now he has to convince Anna that he can love this baby who is biologically neither his nor hers.

On sale 7th December 2001

Available at most branches of WH Smith, Tesco, Martins, Borders, Eason, Sainsbury's and most good paperback bookshops.

1101/03b

1101/59/MB22

MILLS & BOON

Christmas
with a Latin Lover

Three brand-new stories

Lynne Graham
Penny Jordan
Lucy Gordon

Published 19th October

*Available at most branches of WH Smith,
Tesco, Martins, Borders, Eason, Sainsbury's,
and most good paperback bookshops.*

FREE!

4 Books
and a surprise gift!

We would like to take this opportunity to thank you for reading this Mills & Boon® book by offering you the chance to take FOUR more specially selected titles from the Medical Romance™ series absolutely FREE! We're also making this offer to introduce you to the benefits of the Reader Service™—

- ★ FREE home delivery
- ★ FREE gifts and competitions
- ★ FREE monthly Newsletter
- ★ Books available before they're in the shops
- ★ Exclusive Reader Service discounts

Accepting these FREE books and gift places you under no obligation to buy; you may cancel at any time, even after receiving your free shipment. Simply complete your details below and return the entire page to the address below. *You don't even need a stamp!*

YES! Please send me 4 free Medical Romance books and a surprise gift. I understand that unless you hear from me, I will receive 6 superb new titles every month for just £2.49 each, postage and packing free. I am under no obligation to purchase any books and may cancel my subscription at any time. The free books and gift will be mine to keep in any case.

M1ZEB

Ms/Mrs/Miss/Mr ....Initials..
                                                                          BLOCK CAPITALS PLEASE

Surname...

Address..

....

....Postcode ....

Send this whole page to:
UK: The Reader Service, FREEPOST CN8I, Croydon, CR9 3WZ
EIRE: The Reader Service, PO Box 4546, Kilcock, County Kildare (stamp required)

Offer not valid to current Reader Service subscribers to this series. We reserve the right to refuse an application and applicants must be aged 18 years or over. Only one application per household. Terms and prices subject to change without notice. Offer expires 31st May 2002. As a result of this application, you may receive offers from other carefully selected companies. If you would prefer not to share in this opportunity please write to The Data Manager at the address above.

Mills & Boon® is a registered trademark owned by Harlequin Mills & Boon Limited.
Medical Romance™ is being used as a trademark.